AB

Barbara Cartland, the ~~~~~~~~~~~~~~~~~~~~~~~~~~~~~~~
who is also an historia~~~~~~~~~~~~~~~~~~~~~~~~~~~~~~
and television persona~~~~~~~~~~~~~~~~~~~~~~~~~~~~~
sold over 600 million c~p.~~ ~.. ~... ~..~ ...~.. world.

She has also had many historical works published and has written four autobiographies as well as the biographies of her mother and that of her brother, Ronald Cartland, who was the first Member of Parliament to be killed in the last war. This book has a preface by Sir Winston Churchill and has just been published with an introduction by the late Sir Arthur Bryant.

"Love at the Helm" a novel written with the help and inspiration of the late Earl Mountbatten of Burma, Great Uncle of His Royal Highness The Prince of Wales, is being sold for the Mountbatten Memorial Trust.

She has broken the world record for the last seventeen years by writing an average of twenty-three books a year. In the Guinness Book of Records she is listed as the world's top-selling author.

In 1978 she sang an Album of Love Songs with the Royal Philharmonic Orchestra.

In private life Barbara Cartland, who is a Dame of Grace of the Order of St. John of Jerusalem, Chairman of the St. John Council in Hertfordshire and Deputy President of the St. John Ambulance Brigade, has fought for better conditions and salaries for Midwives and Nurses.

She championed the cause for the Elderly in 1956 invoking a Government Enquiry into the "Housing Conditions of Old People".

In 1962 she had the Law of England changed so that Local Authorities had to provide camps for their own Gypsies. This has meant that since then thousands and thousands of Gypsy children have been able to go to School which they had never been able to do in the past, as their caravans were moved every twenty-four hours by the Police.

There are now fourteen camps in Hertfordshire and Barbara Cartland has her own Romany Gypsy Camp called Barbaraville by the Gypsies.

Her designs "Decorating with Love" are being sold all over the U.S.A. and the National Home Fashions League made her in 1981, "Woman of Achievement".

Barbara Cartland's book "Getting Older, Growing Younger" has been published in Great Britain and the U.S.A. and her fifth Cookery Book, "The Romance of Food" is now being used by the House of Commons.

In 1984 she received at Kennedy Airport, America's Bishop Wright Air Industry Award for her contribution to the development of aviation. In 1931 she and two R.A.F. Officers thought of, and carried the first aeroplane-towed glider air-mail.

During the War she was Chief Lady Welfare Officer in Bedfordshire looking after 20,000 Service men and women. She thought of having a pool of Wedding Dresses at the War Office so a Service Bride could hire a gown for the day.

She bought 1,000 secondhand gowns without coupons for the A.T.S., the W.A.A.F.s and the W.R.E.N.S. In 1945 Barbara Cartland received the Certificate of Merit from Eastern Command.

In 1964 Barbara Cartland founded the National Association for Health of which she is the President, as a front for all the Health Stores and for any product made as alternative medicine.

This has now a £500,000,000 turnover a year, with one third going in export.

In January 1988 she received "La Medaille de Vermeil de la Ville de Paris", (The Gold Medal of Paris). This is the highest award to be given by the City of Paris for ACHIEVEMENT – 25 million books sold in France.

In March 1988 Barbara Cartland was asked by the Indian Government to open their Health Resort outside Delhi. This is almost the largest Health Resort in the world.

Barbara Cartland was received with great enthusiasm by her fans, who also fêted her at a Reception in the City and she received the gift of an embossed plate from the Government.

Barbara Cartland was made a Dame of the Order of the British Empire in the 1991 New Year's Honours List, by Her Majesty The Queen for her contribution to literature and for her work for the Community.

AWARDS

1945   Received Certificate of Merit, Eastern Command.

1953   Made a Commander of the Order of St John of Jerusalem. Invested by H.R.H. The Duke of Gloucester at Buckingham Palace.

1972   Invested as Dame of Grace of the Order of St John in London by The Lord Prior, Lord Cacia.

1981   Receives "Achiever of the Year" from the National Home Furnishing Association in Colorado Springs, U.S.A.

1984   Receives Bishop Wright Air Industry Award at Kennedy Airport, for inventing the aeroplane-towed Glider.

1988   Receives from Monsieur Chirac, The Prime Minister, the Gold Medal of the City of Paris, at the Hôtel de la Ville, Paris, for selling 25 million books and giving a lot of employment.

1991   Invested as Dame of the Order of The British Empire, by H.M. The Queen at Buckingham Palace, for her contribution to literature.

A ROYAL REBUKE

Lord Victor Brooke has displeased Her Majesty Queen Victoria by making love to one of her Ladies-in-Waiting.

He is rebuked not in words but by being sent at the height of the Season to accompany the eighteen-year-old Princess Sydella on her journey to Zararis to marry King Stephan.

His Majesty has asked for an English bride as protection against the infiltration of the Russians.

In order to save his face, Lord Victor pretends to his friends that he is going on a Secret Mission.

This proves to be truer than he thinks.

He had expected to be bored on the Battleship that is taking the Princess to Zararis, but instead he finds he is enjoying it more every day.

How he saves the Princess from being killed at sea.

How he saves her again when they arrive in Zararis.

How the Princess marries the King, is all told in this exciting story of love and intrigue, the 509th book by Barbara Cartland.

BARBARA CARTLAND

A Royal Rebuke

Mandarin

A Mandarin Paperback

A ROYAL REBUKE

First published in Great Britain 1996
by Mandarin Paperbacks
an imprint of Reed International Books Ltd
Michelin House, 81 Fulham Road, London SW3 6RB
and Auckland, Melbourne, Singapore and Toronto

Copyright © Cartland Promotions 1996

The author has asserted her moral rights

A CIP catalogue record for this title
is available from the British Library
ISBN 0 7493 1273 4

Printed and bound in Great Britain
by Cox & Wyman Ltd, Reading, Berkshire

AUTHOR'S NOTE

Tsar Alexander III who came to the throne of Russia in 1881 when he was thirty-six years old was a giant.

He was very proud of his physical strength.

He could tear a pack of cards in half, break a rod over his knees and was known to crush a silver rouble with his bare hands.

He was German but he had the enigmatic look of a Russian peasant. This was how he liked to think of himself, so he grew a beard and wore the baggy trousers and checked blouses of the muzhiks.

He was furious, in fact was reported as "burning with indignation" when he thought that Russia had failed in her mission to dominate the Balkans and seize control of the Straits. If this happened it would have given her access to the Mediterranean.

He, however, refused to give in and stubbornly continued to pursue the same goal. He was determined to establish subservient governments in Serbia and Greece.

As it was impossible for Russia to afford another war the Emperor kept his troops home. Yet throughout his reign he waged the first, concerned 'cold war' in history.

De Giers his Foreign Minister encouraged Russian revolutionaries to act as agents in stirring up trouble for the established regimes of the Balkans.

Posing as Icon Sellers Russian undercover men wandered through Serbia arranging subversive cells. Officials of the Russian Embassy paid crowds to stage riots and in the Eastern Rumelian section of Bulgaria, Russian Army Officers opened gymnasiums.

They sounded attractive to the populus but the Officers drilled boys and girls in guerrilla warfare.

CHAPTER ONE
1888

Lord Victor Brooke arrived at Windsor Castle feeling like a School-boy ordered to the Head-master's Study.

He was well aware that he was in disgrace.

More important, more distinguished and older men than he had trembled before they faced Queen Victoria.

It was just bad luck, he thought, that he should have run into trouble.

It had happened last week when he was staying at the Castle for what had been an extremely boring dinner.

It was being given in honour of the Ambassador of a small, unimportant European country.

Lord Victor had yawned his way through the meal.

He had a pompous politician on one side of him, and the Ambassador's rather plain wife on the other.

He was well aware that he had been invited because not only was the Queen his Godmother, but also she liked handsome men.

He would have been very stupid, which he was not, if he had not been aware that he was extremely good-looking.

He seldom made love to a woman who, when she saw him undressed did not compare him to a Greek god.

As the third son of the Duke of Droxbrooke, Lord Victor was welcome in every house of importance in the country.

He was invited to all the Balls, Receptions and dinner-parties that were given for the younger generation.

It was true that ambitious Mothers did not consider him a great matrimonial catch.

With two older brothers, there was little chance of his becoming the Duke.

At the same time, the Droxbrookes were one of the oldest and most distinguished families in England.

It was considered a privilege to be counted as one of their friends.

Lord Victor however was not interested in debutantes or, for that matter, in getting married at all.

He enjoyed life enormously, pursued by or, as he preferred to think, pursuing the beautiful women who surrounded the Prince of Wales.

They were discreetly, but regularly, unfaithful to their husbands.

It was the Prince of Wales who had made it acceptable for a Gentleman to have an *affaire-de-coeur* with a lady of his own class.

Society had welcomed this new attitude with delight.

Husbands were expected to 'turn a blind eye' to their wives' infidelities as long as they were discreet.

There must be no question of their being talked

about outside the closed circle of what was known as 'The Marlborough House Set'.

Lord Victor found it easy to go from *Boudoir* to *Boudoir*.

This was because he was not only handsome, but also charming.

It was considered a 'feather in her cap', if a Beauty had him in attendance, if only for a short time.

Whatever the Marlborough House Set felt amongst themselves, they were acutely aware of the propriety that regulated life at Windsor Castle.

The Queen upheld the almost obsessive morality of the late-lamented Prince Consort.

Last week, the boredom of the dinner had made Lord Victor turn his eyes in the direction of the only attractive Lady-in-Waiting to Her Majesty.

The Countess of Weldon was about the same age as himself.

When their eyes met across the Dining-Room table he knew that she was finding her dinner-partner as deadly as he found his.

Later the Gentlemen joined the Ladies in the Drawing-Room and he managed to reach her side.

When she smiled up at him there was an undoubted invitation in her eyes and a provocative pout to her lips.

It was a look he knew all too well.

In fact he found it hard to remember any occasion when a woman had not looked at him in that way.

He paid the Countess a compliment, and she pretended to be both surprised and embarrassed by it.

It was however only pretence.

From that moment Lord Victor thought the party was a little less unbearable than it had been before.

Because the Queen's eyes were on him, he contrived to have conversations with several other guests.

Yet when he spoke to the Countess again after the Queen had retired, he knew what was expected of him.

Windsor Castle was a rabbit-warren of passages, corridors and stairs.

They had defeated a great many visitors over the years.

A story concerning one Gentleman had been repeated in every Club in St. James's.

He had tried to find his bed-room, but failed.

Because he had dined well he sat down on a sofa and fell asleep.

He was discovered by an hysterical house-maid early the next morning who thought he was a burglar.

It was a story that had pursued the unfortunate man for the rest of his life.

There were a great number of other tales, including one about a guest who opened the door of what he thought was his own bed-room.

What he found was Her Majesty sitting at a dressing-table with her hair down.

Lord Victor however knew Windsor Castle better than most people.

The Queen had patronised him ever since he was a small boy.

He had then found it amusing to explore the Castle, to climb up the towers and slide down the banisters.

Now he was thinking that a definitely redeeming feature about this visit would be the Countess of Weldon.

When finally after only a slight hesitation he found her bed-room, it was, he realised, uncomfortably near to Her Majesty's.

It was in a part of the Castle which was usually reserved for the Ladies-in-Waiting.

However when he opened the door, then locked it behind him, he was not thinking of the risk he was taking.

He was thinking only of Nancy Weldon.

She was in fact very lovely with her hair falling over her shoulders.

There was just enough candlelight in the room to reveal her white skin and the curves of her breasts beneath a diaphanous nightgown.

Lord Victor reached the bed and stood looking down at her.

"You are very lovely, Nancy!" he said softly.

"That is what I want you to think," she answered and held out her arms.

. . . .

It was two o'clock before Lord Victor thought it was time for him to return to his own room.

But Nancy, who he had found was, as he had expected, insatiable, clung to him.

"I had better go," he told her. "I do not want to risk stumbling into a soldier coming on duty, or one of those tiresome Night-watchmen who prowl about the passages."

"I cannot bear you to leave me," she said softly. "When shall I see you again?"

It was a question he thought every woman asked him when he was about to leave her.

He knew however that if she was tied to her duties at Windsor Castle, it would be difficult for them to meet.

"We must think about it," he answered.

She started to protest, but he rose, put on his dressing-gown and picked up the candle with which he had lit his way from his part of the Castle to this.

He bent to kiss her hand saying:

"Good-night, Nancy, and thank you for making me very happy."

It was something he had said a great many times.

He did it with a grace which invariably thrilled the woman to whom he was speaking.

"Do let us meet again soon!" the Countess pleaded.

By this time Lord Victor was walking across the room.

He turned to smile at her as he opened the door.

Cautiously he looked both left and right before he emerged from the room.

Everything was quiet.

He shut the door softly and walked quickly down the passage.

It was as he turned left that he bumped violently into someone coming from the other direction.

It was a woman.

By the light of his candle, and the one she carried, he saw it was the Marchioness of Belgrade.

She was wearing an elaborate lace-edged dressing-gown and a lace cap.

Lord Victor parted his lips to apologise, but she said sharply:

16

"Lord Victor! What are you doing here at this hour of the night?"

"I am afraid I lost my way," Lord Victor replied. "These corridors are a complete maze!"

As he spoke he walked on quickly, hoping the Marchioness had not seen from which direction he had come.

Yet he was sure as he left Windsor Castle later that morning that what had happened had already been relayed to the Queen.

He had not communicated with Nancy Weldon since leaving for the simple reason that his letter would have to go to the Castle.

When he received a summons four days later to an audience with the Queen, he knew he was in trouble.

Because he was apprehensive he made enquiries about the Marchioness.

He learned, as he might have expected, that she was the oldest of the Ladies-in-Waiting.

She was therefore more or less in charge of those who were younger and certainly more attractive than herself.

Lord Victor learnt that in fact she was thoroughly disliked in the Castle.

But that did not make his position any better.

An *Aide-de-Camp* greeted him at the doorway.

He escorted him along the twisting passages and up the stairs to the Queen's private apartments.

Lord Victor knew his way perfectly well.

However he realised that the way he was being received indicated better than words that he was in trouble.

If the *Aide-de-Camp* had been a young man,

he might have asked him confidentially what was afoot.

But he was an older man who obviously had no desire to make himself pleasant or to appear friendly.

Lord Victor therefore walked along behind him without speaking.

There was the usual pause before the Queen's Room could be approached.

A whispered conversation took place with another *Aide-de-Camp* who was on duty.

This was a procedure which, Lord Victor thought, usually amused him.

He thought it was a lot of nonsense, just to impress visitors, whoever they were.

Certainly it created an atmosphere of awe and respect.

Now, as far as he himself was concerned, he could not help feeling a little apprehensive.

As the *Aide-de-Camp* who had entered the room to announce him came out walking backwards, he said:

"Her Majesty will see you now."

It was a room Lord Victor knew all too well.

There were the silver-framed photographs which travelled with the Queen wherever she went.

There was an aspidistra in a corner, and anti-macassars over the tops of the chairs.

Amid a mêlée of small tables laden with *objets d'art* was the Queen herself, wearing black.

She was small in stature, but overwhelming in authority and importance.

Her Majesty had celebrated the 50th year of her reign.

Lord Victor could not help thinking of the un-precedented developments in travel, communication, education and the acquisition of political power that had happened during that time.

She now reigned over an enormous Empire covering three-quarters of the world's land surface.

At School, he remembered, it had been marked in red on the maps.

Amazingly enough, this was what one small woman had achieved.

When she came to the Throne in 1837, she had said:

"I will be good."

Now, Lord Victor thought, much of the world bowed down to her.

It was not surprising that she was awe-inspiring.

Lord Victor walked slowly towards the Queen and saw that she was looking at him without a smile.

Yet, when he bowed and kissed first her hand, as her Godson, then her cheek, he thought her eyes softened.

"I sent for you, Victor," she said in her clear, slightly hard voice, "for I have a duty for you to perform."

"I am honoured, Ma'am," Lord Victor replied.

At the same time, he was well aware that this was going to be a punishment.

"I have thought for some time," the Queen continued, "that you should do something for your country, rather than just enjoy yourself, as I understand you have been doing – lately."

There was just a pause before the last word.

"Of course," Lord Victor answered. "I shall be

delighted to do anything Your Majesty commands."

That was far from the truth.

Nevertheless, he had no alternative but to be pleasant about anything that was suggested.

"I have always believed that travel enriches the mind," the Queen said, "and I think, Victor, you have not been abroad for some time."

"I did go to Paris two months ago," Lord Victor replied, "but it was only a short visit."

"Paris!" the Queen exclaimed.

It was obvious she was thinking not of the cultural riches of France, but what he had been doing in Paris, and with whom he had spent his time there.

Her eyes hardened as she said:

"I have no wish to criticise, but what I hear of Paris at the moment makes me think it is not the right place for a young man to spend his time – or his money."

Lord Victor could not help wondering which *Cocotte*'s behaviour had been relayed to the Queen.

He could understand all too well what her reaction would have been.

"What I am asking you to do at the moment," the Queen went on, "is to visit a country which is very different in every way from anywhere you have been before, and which needs the protection of Great Britain and my Empire."

There was an undoubted note of pride in the Queen's voice as she said the last words.

Lord Victor was aware that the Queen's policy was to extend her protection to almost every small country in Europe.

She married her relatives to their Kings and

Crown Princes so that they could rule under the protection of the Union Jack.

He remembered someone saying at Windsor Castle last week that there were nearly twenty thrones in this category.

He wondered if there could be many more of them.

As if she knew what Lord Victor was thinking, the Queen said:

"I am sending you, Victor, to Zararis."

Lord Victor looked at her blankly.

"Zararis, Ma'am?" he repeated.

"It is a small country," the Queen said quickly, "but of importance because it is on the Aegean Sea, bordered by countries into which the Russians are infiltrating."

She paused before she added sharply:

"You must be aware of what we feel about Russia at the moment."

"Yes, of course, Ma'am," Lord Victor agreed.

"King Stephen has asked that I should provide him with a wife. I am therefore sending him Princess Sydella of Troilus, and you will be escorting her to Zararis as my representative at the wedding."

Lord Victor was astounded.

Such an assignment was traditionally carried out by a much older man, and usually a Statesman.

At the same time he was aware that she was, in fact, rebuking and punishing him very effectively.

He knew how exceptionally boring such a duty would be.

Princess Sydella, whoever she might be, was, he was sure, young, dull and plain.

She was doubtless a member of the Saxe-Coburg

family whom the Queen treated as her own.

She would be accompanied by two Ladies-in-Waiting, the Zararian Ambassador and his wife, and perhaps an elderly Statesman.

And lastly, himself.

He could almost see Her Majesty concocting it all in her mind.

A month or two of boredom for him would be the equivalent of being sent to prison, or purgatory.

He thought there was a look of triumph in the Queen's expression as she waited to see his reaction.

He was however determined not to let her know that she had succeeded in demoralising him.

"That sounds extremely interesting, Ma'am," he said, "and I will of course do my best to represent my country in exactly the way Your Majesty would wish, and make King Stephan realise how extremely fortunate he is in enjoying Your Majesty's support and your generosity in finding him a Bride."

"You will leave in three days' time," the Queen said. "The Princess is travelling to Zararis by sea in H.M.S. *Victorious*."

"I can only thank Your Majesty for being so exceedingly gracious," Lord Victor said, "as to honour me with what will undoubtedly be a most enjoyable and exciting duty."

He forced a note of sincerity into his voice which he was sure surprised the Queen.

Just for a moment he thought she was wondering if she had made a mistake.

Then she said sharply:

"You will be given all particulars about Zararis, which is very important, by the Prime Minister the

Marquess of Salisbury, and on your return I would like a report on that country, which is at least sensible enough to have asked for our protection."

Her lips tightened before she added:

"I understand that Russia is becoming more and more menacing in the Balkans, and we must do our best to keep them within their own boundaries."

"Yes, of course, Ma'am," Lord Victor agreed. "I will make it clear that if Zararis is under the protection of the British Flag, it is a matter of 'Hands Off!' There must be no question of their inciting the Zararians into rebellion."

He was well aware that this had happened in a number of Balkan States.

The British Government had been extremely perturbed about it.

There had been discussions in Parliament, and British Battleships had been sent to the Aegean Sea as a warning to the Russians not to go too far.

"I will see you on your return," the Queen said.

Lord Victor knew that he was dismissed.

He therefore kissed her hand and again her cheek before he backed out of the room.

He thought as he found himself outside that at least he had managed to hold his own.

Yet he was aware that the Queen thought she had taught him a lesson which he would not forget in a hurry.

She knew perfectly well what it meant to him to be sent to Zararis in May.

He would miss the Balls and parties that took place every day during the Season.

He would also miss the Polo at which he excelled,

the racing at Royal Ascot which took place in the second week of June, and a great number of other amusements.

He had already accepted dozens of invitations.

He wondered as he left Windsor Castle whether he could plead illness.

Perhaps a miracle or a lucky accident might save him at the last minute!

Then perhaps H.M.S. *Victorious* would sail without him.

He knew however that if he really defied the Queen it would be something she would never forgive, or forget.

The only thing he could do was to pretend that her rebuke and intended punishment was something he in fact enjoyed.

He would have to deceive not only her, but also his friends.

That was going to be the most difficult task.

He was well aware they all knew that to escort some unimportant and unfledged, half-witted young Royalty to the altar would be boring beyond words.

None of the younger members of White's Club would find it anything but a yawn.

"I am damned if I will have them laughing at me!" Lord Victor told himself.

All the same, he had no one to blame but himself, and of course the unmistakable allurement of Nancy Weldon.

As he drove towards London he thought he would miss the new pair of horses he was driving in his Chaise.

They had been expensive, but he thought they were undoubtedly worth what he had paid for them.

At the same time, it meant he had to economise on other things.

As a third son, his allowance was comparatively small.

It was usual in great families that everything was concentrated on the oldest son who would eventually succeed to the Peerage.

It had never particularly worried Lord Victor.

Yet he sometimes asked himself how, unless he married an heiress, he would ever be able to support a family in the way to which he was accustomed.

He had meant when he left Oxford to go into the Household Cavalry.

Although they would have welcomed him there because it was the Family Regiment, it was costly even for a Subaltern.

Lord Victor therefore just availed himself of Droxbrooke House in Park Lane, and spent his time doing what he enjoyed.

He played Polo, and was in demand by some of the best teams.

He enjoyed a game of Squash almost every day because it kept him fit.

He rode his own horses and those of his friends, both in London and in the country.

It was inevitable that he should find that women hunted him even more effectively than he hunted a fox with the best Packs during the Winter.

No one could pretend that this was not enjoyable.

In fact he had until now found his life a 'bed of roses'.

It was typical of the Queen, he thought, to know that he would hate leaving London when it was at its most amusing for any unattached young man.

Yet he was determined that no one should know that he was put out by her command.

He would also pretend on his return that the whole journey had been an exciting adventure.

It did not take him long to reach London from Windsor.

He went straight to White's Club.

As he walked into the Morning-Room he found, as he expected, several of his friends were there.

"Where have you been?" one of them asked.

"To Windsor Castle," Lord Victor replied.

"Good Lord! What for? I thought you were there only last week!"

"I was," Lord Victor said.

He seated himself in one of the leather arm-chairs before he added:

"Her Majesty felt compelled to see me again!"

There was just a touch of laughter about his voice, and one of his closest friends said:

"You are up to something, Victor! What did the Queen want you for?"

"You will hardly believe it," Lord Victor replied, "but I am to go to Zararis! It really is one of the most exciting things that has happened to me for a long time!"

Another man who was listening enquired:

"Where the hell *is* Zararis? What do you do there?"

Lord Victor lowered his voice.

"This is confidential," he said, "and of course you must not repeat it to a soul, but actually I will be on a secret mission!"

CHAPTER TWO

Lord Victor was asked to be at Downing Street at ten o'clock.

He drove there in his Chaise.

He was thinking that once again he felt like a troublesome pupil going to the Headmaster's Study.

He was however a great admirer of the Marquess of Salisbury, who had been for many years the dominating influence in British Foreign Policy.

Lord Victor knew, from what he had heard and read, that the Marquess, as a younger Statesman, had been a brilliant administrator at the India Office.

He was aware that in particular he was a high authority on Russian Affairs and the Eastern question.

When Foreign Secretary he had played a most influential part in the Congress of Berlin ten years ago.

This, Lord Victor realised, linked up with what the Queen had said about Russia.

He wished now that he had been older when there had been an international crisis which had been caused by the Grand Duke Nicholas's march towards Constantinople.

The Russian Army were deterred from storming

the City only by the intervention of Britain in sending the Navy up the Dardanelles.

"If I am to keep up my pretence that I am on a Secret Mission," Lord Victor told himself, "I shall have to mug up my knowledge of the political situation in the Balkans."

He however appeared carefree and in high spirits when he arrived at Downing Street.

He was shown into the Marquess of Salisbury's office, who rose to his feet and held out his hand.

"It is nice to see you, Victor," he said in his deep voice. "I hope your Father is well?"

"He is well enough when he is at home," Lord Victor replied, "but he resents having to come to London, and prefers to stay in the country."

"I can understand his feelings," the Marquess smiled. "Do sit down."

Lord Victor settled himself in the chair on the other side of the Marquess's desk.

He thought that the Statesman was beginning to look his fifty-eight years.

At the same time his appearance was very distinguished.

The hair above his high intelligent forehead was going grey and the same applied to his short beard.

The Marquess cleared his throat.

"Her Majesty has told me, rather surprisingly, if you will forgive me saying so, that she is sending you to Zararis with the prospective Queen."

"The Queen informed me," Lord Victor answered, "that I am to go to the wedding and see that the Union Jack is flying over Zararis."

He spoke mockingly.

The Marquess did not reply, and after a moment Lord Victor added:

"I will be frank with you, My Lord. I have no idea where Zararis is, or why, apart from the fact that they want our protection, it is of any importance."

"That is what I will tell you," the Marquess of Salisbury said, "because, Victor, Zararis is extremely important at this moment."

Lord Victor raised his eye-brows and the Marquess of Salisbury explained as if he was teaching a reluctant pupil:

"Zararis lies on the Aegean coast between Macedonia and Eastern Rumelia, which three years ago voted for incorporation with Bulgaria as its Southern province."

"Now my Geography is coming back to me," Lord Victor said. "I remember, unless I am mistaken, that this region is at the top of the Aegean Sea."

"That is right," the Marquess agreed, "and although it is only a small country, it is vitally important at the moment to keep it independent and out of Russian hands."

He saw from the expression on Lord Victor's face that he did not quite understand why and he went on:

"When Alexander III, the present Tsar, came to the Throne seven years ago, he burned with indignation that Russia had failed in what he thought to be her destiny to dominate the Balkans and have control of the Straits."

He glanced at Lord Victor and added:

"You realise that would have given him access to the Mediterranean?"

"Yes, of course," Lord Victor agreed hastily.

"The Tsar was also determined to establish subservient Governments in Serbia and Greece."

"Does he still want that?" Lord Victor asked. "He must realise that he cannot afford another war!"

He was remembering what somebody had told him.

On the failure of Russia's effort towards the conquest of Constantinople Prince Gorchakov said bitterly:

"We have sacrificed 100,000 picked soldiers and 100-millions of money for nothing!"

"Alexander has been wise enough," the Marquess went on, "to keep his troops at home, which has made some foolish Statesmen in Europe refer to him as 'The Tsar Peacemaker'!"

"I suppose he is nothing of the sort," Lord Victor said.

The Marquess sighed.

"He is waging," he said, "one of the strangest wars in history."

"How?" Lord Victor asked.

"His Foreign Minister, de Giers," the Marquess explained, "has planted Russian spies all over the Balkans to act as agents in starting up trouble in the established Régimes."

Lord Victor sat up in his chair.

This was something he had certainly not heard before.

"Russian undercover men," the Prime Minister went on, "disguised as icon-sellers, wander through Serbia setting up subversive cells."

"I can hardly believe it!" Lord Victor exclaimed.

"It is true," the Marquess answered, "and the

Russian Embassy Officials pay crowds to stage riots."

"Is anyone aware of this?" Lord Victor asked.

"I am aware of it," the Marquess replied, "and I can only pray that things will not go too far, or we shall have to intervene."

He looked down at his desk before he said:

"I have only to-day learnt that Russian Army Officers in the Eastern Rumelian section of Bulgaria have opened Gymnasiums where they drill boys and girls in guerrilla warfare."

Because it seemed so inconceivable, Lord Victor was silent.

Then the Marquess went on:

"I am telling you this, Victor, entirely confidentially because I need your help."

Lord Victor just stared at him and the Marquess said slowly:

"I have been wanting for some time to get an entirely unbiased report from Zararis on what is happening in that country and, of course, the larger countries around it. But it has not been easy because, to be frank, the Zararian Officials themselves are old, and I have a feeling that like ostriches they bury their heads in the sand."

"I will naturally find out all I can," Lord Victor said, "but I had hoped not to stay long."

The Prime Minister's eyes twinkled.

"I thought Her Majesty must have some reason for appointing you when I had already arranged for Lord Ludlow to escort the Princess. It is something he has done on similar occasions."

"To tell you the truth," Lord Victor said, "Her Majesty is not very pleased with me at the moment.

I am therefore being sent abroad at a time when it is personally extremely inconvenient for me."

"I thought that would be the explanation," the Marquess said. "I have known you, Victor, ever since you were a small boy, and I think you have been wasting your brains the last few years. I remember your Father telling me how well you had done at Eton, and that you came down from Oxford with a First."

"You flatter me," Lord Victor said, "but nobody since then has been particularly interested in my brain."

The Marquess laughed.

"That is exactly what I imagined, and very beautiful women do not provide the right stimulus for that part of your anatomy."

He looked down again at the notes on his desk and said:

"Now, seriously, I want you to use your brain while appearing to those with whom you travel and whom you meet in Zararis to be no more than an escort and companion to the Princess."

Lord Victor was thinking this was most extraordinary!

Just to impress his friends and prevent them from laughing at him, he had invented the idea of a Secret Mission.

Now apparently he was actually to undertake one.

As if the Marquess was following his thoughts he said:

"I will give you what particulars I have of what is happening in Zararis. I want you to read them carefully, commit them to memory, and destroy the papers when you have done so."

"This is really cloak and dagger drama!" Lord Victor remarked.

"Let me assure you, my dear boy, it is actually very serious," the Marquess said. "One unwary step, any inkling you afford to the Russians of what you are about, might quite easily end in an 'unfortunate accident'."

"Now you are frightening me!" Lord Victor protested. "At the same time, I am intrigued."

"I thought you would be," the Marquess answered. "And now let me tell you what is ostensibly your duty, unless Her Majesty has already done so."

"She told me that you would supply all the details and merely informed me that I was to escort a young woman of whom I have never heard to marry King Stephan."

"That is right," the Marquess answered. "Princess Sydella is the daughter of Prince Alexis of Troilus."

He realised that Lord Victor was looking blank and explained:

"Troilus is a Greek island that had its own Principality since the liberation of Greece and the Aegean from Turkish rule. Then there was not exactly a Revolution, but a take-over by a Party that was anti-Royal. Prince Alexis escaped to England with his life."

Lord Victor was listening intently and the Marquess went on:

"He was an exceedingly good-looking and charming man, and although he had no money and no prospects, he fell madly in love with the daughter of the Duke of Hauchester."

"Who of course was English," Lord Victor remarked, "but not Royal."

"On the contrary," the Marquess answered, "she had a distant relationship to Her Majesty through her Mother. The Duchess was a relative of the Duke of Cambridge, Uncle to the Queen."

He paused before he added:

"Her Majesty is Godmother to the Princess Sydella, just as she is Godmother to you."

"Well, that is one thing we have in common," Lord Victor said with a cynical note in his voice.

He was thinking that however exciting things might be when they arrived in Zararis, the voyage would undoubtedly be as boring as he expected.

"Prince Alexis was killed out hunting five years ago," the Marquess was saying, "and Princess Louise has lived very quietly since his death in a small house on her Father's estate. As you are aware, the Hauchesters live in Northumberland and I doubt if the Princess has ever been to London."

Lord Victor wondered, in that case, what they would have to talk about.

The Marquess went on:

"I know that Her Majesty has found it very hard to find an answer to King Stephan's plea for an English wife. In fact the only young woman available at this particular moment is Princess Sydella."

The way he spoke made Lord Victor realise he was sorry for the Princess.

He therefore somewhat belatedly asked:

"How old is King Stephan?"

"Getting on for sixty, if not older," the Marquess answered.

"And the Princess?" Lord Victor enquired.

"She is just eighteen."

For a moment Lord Victor did not speak.

Then he said:

"Yet Her Majesty thinks it will be a suitable marriage? Quite frankly, I find the idea repulsive!"

The Marquess sat back in his chair.

"I agree with you, Victor, but you know as well as I do that they are merely pawns in the game. The disparity in their ages of course makes it impossible to imagine that two such people can possibly be together."

He sighed before he continued:

"However, what is important is that the Russians will realise, as you have already said, that they must keep their hands off Zararis. That, diplomatically, is what concerns us."

Lord Victor could think of no answer to this and merely asked:

"Will I meet the Princess before I leave?"

"I understand," the Marquess replied, "that she is at the moment in the country saying good-bye to her Grandfather and will, when she reaches London, go straight to the ship."

"H.M.S. *Victorious*!" Lord Victor said sarcastically. "Well, I can only hope, My Lord, that from your point of view the voyage will be a success."

"I hope so too," the Marquess said quietly. "But do not forget, Victor, what is of prime importance. I am relying on you to use your eyes and ears, and above all that brain of yours, to bring me back a report which I can trust on what is going on in Zararis beneath all the pomp and glamour with which you will be received."

"I will do my best," Lord Victor replied, "but you must not be disappointed if I find there is nothing untoward."

"On the contrary, I shall be most relieved," the Marquess answered. "At the same time I am extremely glad that you are going to Zararis."

"Which is more than I am," Lord Victor murmured.

"Although you may find it irksome," the Marquess continued, "you may save a great many lives and help us to prevent the Tsar from realising his ambitions, with which he is completely obsessed."

"I have always heard that he is an exceedingly unpleasant man," Lord Victor said, "and, unless I am mistaken, I believe he is mean to the point of madness."

He was searching his mind as he spoke to remember what he had heard or read about Tsar Alexander III.

The Marquess nodded.

"You are right about that," he said. "I am told he wears his clothes until they are threadbare and his shoes until they fall off his feet."

Lord Victor laughed and the Marquess went on:

"But his cruelty to the Jews has been unprecedented in the whole of History! He has killed thousands, and it was estimated recently that 235,000 Jewish families had been forced out of Russia into Western Europe."

"Then the Tsar certainly deserves any bad luck that is coming his way," Lord Victor remarked.

"That is what I feel," the Marquess answered,

"so let me, Victor, wish you the best of luck on what must appear to the outside world as a formal Royal duty, but which you and I know is something very different."

He rose as he spoke.

"Take care of yourself, my dear boy. Put nothing in writing, and do not talk in your sleep!"

Lord Victor laughed, as he was meant to do.

The Marquess put his hand affectionately on Lord Victor's shoulder and walked with him to the door.

As they reached it he said quietly, almost as if he was afraid someone was listening:

"Take no risks, and remember we are fighting a giant octopus that wants to gobble up the Balkan States, one by one."

He did not wait for Lord Victor to reply, but opened the door.

As he did so he said in a very different voice:

"Good-bye, Victor. Give my good wishes to your Father and say I hope I shall be seeing him very soon."

"I know, My Lord, he will look forward to that," Lord Victor said in the same careless, good-humoured manner.

He was smiling as he walked jauntily towards the front door to where his Chaise was waiting.

Only when he was alone did he wonder if he had been dreaming.

Could it possibly be true that when he had never thought of such a thing except as a joke, he was setting off on what could be an extremely dangerous mission?

"I do not believe it!" he said to himself.

Lord Victor spent the next day saying good-bye to a number of his friends.

He wrote abject apologies for having to refuse a number of invitations he had already accepted.

Then he gave orders to his Valet for what he required on the voyage.

One invitation he regretted refusing more than any other was a house-party being given by the lovely Daisy Brooke, and included the Prince of Wales.

Her husband was later to succeed to the Earldom of Warwick.

Lord Victor knew how enjoyable the house-party would be because Daisy was an outstanding hostess.

She had also arranged for horse-races on her private course at which he was confident of being the winner.

He had found at parties which included the Prince of Wales that the guests were chosen very carefully.

This was so that His Royal Highness should be amused from breakfast to dinner.

It was also well known that he had fallen madly in love with Daisy Brooke.

It was, Lord Victor was told, a very much deeper emotion than he had ever felt for any of the other Beauties who had passed through his hands.

This would, Lord Victor thought, add a spice to the party which would make it unforgettable.

He cancelled his engagements one after the other.

As he did so he could not help wondering if the Marquess was exaggerating the situation in Zararis.

If so, the hush-hush game in which he was to take part would not compensate him for the fun he was missing in England.

However, as he told himself philosophically, it was no use 'kicking against the pricks'.

The following morning, when he had finished breakfast, Lord Victor set off for Tilbury.

He could not help feeling, after what the Prime Minister had said, that he might be saying good-bye to Droxbrooke House for the last time.

His Valet had been surprised when he packed his revolver.

He had also added to his ordinary clothes, garments which did not seem at all appropriate to a Palace.

If he had to creep about dark streets at night, or go underground, he could hardly be wearing his best and more formal attire.

He travelled in his Curricle towards Tilbury followed by his Valet in a Brake with his luggage.

Lord Victor found himself thinking wistfully of the Polo ground at Ranelagh.

That was where he should, this afternoon, be playing a very intense game.

There was also a dinner-party to-night given by one of the great Beauties of the moment, Lady Newman.

The last time they had met she had made it clear that they should 'get to know each other better'.

There was the same glitter in her eyes that there had been in Nancy Weldon's.

It was an invitation he could not misunderstand.

"Damn! Damn! Damn!" he said beneath his breath.

The wheels of the Curricle turned round and round in time to the words.

How, he asked, could he have been such a fool as to get himself in a position where he was leaving everything that was enjoyable?

He would be days and days at sea with no one to talk to, and nothing to look at except the waves.

H.M.S. *Victorious* was alongside the largest Quay at Tilbury.

As Lord Victor looked at her he had a wild desire to turn his horses round and drive away.

Why, just for a whim of the Queen, should he have to waste a month or more of his life?

Why was he not man enough to refuse the Royal Command?

"I am not a soldier, I am not a sailor," he tried to argue. "I am supposed to be a free citizen with no restrictions on my movements."

Yet he knew as the horses came to a standstill that he was only fantasising.

No man would dare to refuse the command of Queen Victoria, however brave they might think themselves to be.

Her Majesty had committed him very effectively to prison.

If it took him two months to work out his sentence, there was nothing he could do about it.

"Look after the horses, Johnson," he said to his groom, "and do not forget to send most of them to the country."

"Aye, Oi'll no' forget, M'Lord," Johnson replied. " 'Ave a good voyage, an' Oi 'opes it's not too rough for ye."

"I hope so too," Lord Victor answered.

He realised as he walked up the gang-plank that he was slightly late.

The rest of the party would have already arrived.

The Captain confirmed that this was correct.

Having greeted Lord Victor, he told a Junior Officer to take His Lordship below.

"I hope, My Lord," he said politely, "that you will join me later on the Bridge, but I now wish to put to sea."

Lord Victor smiled.

"I am sorry, Captain, that I kept you waiting."

"Only a few minutes, My Lord, but it is better to move with the tide, and the sea is calm, thank goodness! It is certainly what the Ladies prefer while we men have to put up with any weather."

"That is true," Lord Victor agreed.

He followed the Junior Officer from the deck and down the companionway.

He was aware that on occasions like this the Captain's private quarters were given up to the most important guest.

The Junior Officers were moved from their comfortable cabins to inferior ones.

This meant that the midshipmen had to accept any hole or corner that was left.

"Would you like to go to your cabin, My Lord?" the Officer conducting him asked.

"I think first," Lord Victor replied, "I should make my apologies to Her Royal Highness. I have just realised that I should have been here in good time to welcome her on her arrival."

The Officer grinned.

"There were plenty of us to do that, My Lord!"

He opened a door as he spoke and Lord Victor went into a low-ceilinged, but large and comfortably furnished room.

It was, he assumed, the Captain's Day-Cabin.

There were a number of people present.

When he appeared an elderly man sprang to his feet.

Lord Victor walked towards him.

"You must forgive me, Your Excellency," he said, "for being a little late. The traffic was heavier than I expected, so I hope you will accept my apologies."

"Of course, My Lord, of course!" the Ambassador replied with a heavy foreign accent. "And now that Your Lordship has arrived, let me introduce you to our party."

He walked across the Cabin as he spoke to where two elderly ladies with grey hair were sitting side by side.

He introduced Lord Victor and they would have risen to their feet, if he had not told them quickly not to move.

They were both Baronesses and spoke English with some difficulty.

Beside them was another man who Lord Victor understood was a Statesman.

He had been sent to represent his Prime Minister on this auspicious occasion.

He spoke practically no English, and Lord Victor realised that he was in fact speaking Greek.

He had studied Classical Greek when he was at Oxford.

He hoped somewhat forlornly that it might help him to understand modern spoken Greek.

There was no one else in the cabin.

As if the Ambassador read his thoughts, he said:

"Her Royal Highness insisted on going on deck to see the ship moving out of dock. I thought we should wait here for your arrival, but perhaps now you would like to join her."

Lord Victor thought there was no hurry.

When the Ambassador offered him a drink he accepted it.

As he did so he said:

"I have only just realised that I did not ask the Marquess of Salisbury what language you speak in Zararis, but I think the gentleman to whom you have just introduced me was speaking Greek."

The Ambassador smiled.

"They have obviously not told you the history of our country."

"I should be interested to hear it," Lord Victor said politely.

"Two centuries ago a number of Greeks were so dissatisfied with the rule of the Turks in Greece that they left and made a new home in Zararis which was then an almost uninhabited region."

Lord Victor was listening, but not with any enthusiasm.

"Over the years," the Ambassador went on, "we have assimilated some of the languages of the adjoining countries with the exception of Turkey. But if, My Lord, you can speak Greek, you will soon understand Zararian, even though it may seem a little strange at first."

"That is certainly good news," Lord Victor said. "I have no wish to miss anything on what I am sure

43

will be a most interesting visit, and I would like to speak to people in their own language."

He was thinking as he spoke that he was fluent in French especially when he was making love.

He could also make himself understood in Italy and Spain.

One language he abominated was German.

It was a relief to learn that that at least would not be a problem in Zararis.

He was thinking however that, after what the Prime Minister had said to him, if he had any sense, or the time, he should have learnt a little Russian.

"What we must do while we are aboard ship," the Ambassador was saying, "is to talk to each other occasionally in Greek. I am sure, My Lord, that if you once learned our ancient and very beautiful language, you will soon pick it up again."

"I think that is an excellent idea," Lord Victor agreed.

As he spoke he heard the engines, which had been turning over quietly, accelerate.

The ship began to move faster.

"I think," he said to the Ambassador, "it would be interesting if we went up on the Bridge and watched the ship move down the river."

"But certainly, My Lord, if that is what you would like," the Ambassador agreed.

They left the Cabin and went up the companionway on to the deck.

Seamen were hurrying about as they walked towards the Bridge.

Even before they actually stepped onto it Lord Victor could hear a woman's voice.

She was talking excitedly.

Then he saw to his astonishment a head of golden hair shining in the sunshine.

He had been so certain that with Greek blood in her the Princess would be dark, as her Father must have been.

For a moment he thought he must have been mistaken and this could not be the Princess.

Perhaps there was another young woman aboard.

Then the Ambassador came forward to say:

"Allow me, Your Royal Highness, to present Lord Victor Brooke, who on Her Majesty Queen Victoria's instructions is accompanying us on the journey to Zararis."

As he was speaking the golden head turned round and Lord Victor found himself looking at Princess Sydella.

She was without exception the most beautiful young woman he had ever seen.

CHAPTER THREE

For a moment, the Princess and Lord Victor just stared at each other.

Then she said as though it burst from her lips:

"Oh, but you are young!"

Even as she spoke she realised what she had said and put her fingers to her mouth.

Lord Victor glanced to see where the Ambassador was.

To his relief the Captain was showing him a chart.

He looked at the Princess who was smiling.

"I am sorry," she whispered, "but it was such a surprise to see you."

"And I am equally surprised on seeing Your Royal Highness," Lord Victor replied.

He realised that she was amused.

She must have guessed that he had been expecting somebody very different.

Her appearance was certainly unpredictable in that she was small and very slim.

Her heart-shaped face seemed to be overwhelmed by the size of her eyes.

Lord Victor had seen a great deal of Greek sculpture.

He knew that the Princess had the features of a Greek goddess.

But surprisingly her hair was fair with traces of gold that was very English.

It complemented her skin which was dazzlingly white.

Lord Victor thought to himself that she combined her Greek and English ancestry very cleverly.

As soon as she had got over her surprise at seeing him, she was talking away excitedly about the voyage.

To her it was obviously an adventure that she had never expected.

She was thrilled with the ship, with the sea, and the journey that lay ahead.

It was impossible, Lord Victor found, not to become caught up in what was to her a dream come true.

"I have always wanted to go to sea," she confided in him, "but I never thought it would be in a Battleship!"

She gave a little laugh before she added in a low voice:

"Or that I should be so important!"

They stayed on the Bridge until the Ambassador suggested there would be coffee waiting for them below.

As it was obviously something he wanted himself, the Princess agreed that they should leave the Bridge.

When they reached the Captain's Day-Cabin the two Ladies-in-Waiting rose as the Princess entered and curtsied to her.

"You should have come up on deck," she told

them. "It is so lovely up there and very exciting to see the ship moving down the river to the sea."

The two Baronesses shivered and Lord Victor asked:

"Did you have a good voyage on the way here?"

"Not very good," one of the Baronesses replied. "In fact it was very rough in the Bay of Biscay and we had to stay in our cabins."

"Well, I hope it is smoother this time," Lord Victor said politely.

He drank the coffee, but refused the biscuits that were served with it.

Then the Princess said eagerly:

"Now can we go back on deck? I do not want to miss anything when we are going down the Straits to the English Channel."

The two Baronesses looked at each other in dismay and Lord Victor said quickly:

"I will look after you, Ma'am. I feel these Ladies might find it difficult to walk as there is already quite a swell."

"Then of course you must stay here," the Princess said to the two elderly women.

It was difficult for Lord Victor not to laugh at the relief on their faces.

The Princess turned towards the door and the Ambassador said to him:

"I feel, My Lord, you can manage without me. I have some rather important letters to write."

"Yes, of course," Lord Victor replied.

As he joined the Princess on the companionway, she said:

"Now that we are free of the 'Watch-dogs', we can enjoy ourselves!"

"Is that your name for them, Ma'am?" Lord Victor enquired.

She smiled and he realised she had a dimple on either side of her mouth.

It made her face even more fascinating than it was when she was serious.

"It is what my Mother told me my Father always called the Ladies-in-Waiting who attended the Queen. When we went to Buckingham Palace they told me what I had to do, exactly as if I were a puppy they were trying to break in."

Lord Victor laughed because he could not help it.

"That is not the sort of thing, Ma'am, you should say at Windsor Castle."

"I was not so stupid as to say it to the Queen!" the Princess answered. "But you must not forget that my existence had only just come to Her Majesty's attention. She made it quite clear that she would not have sent me to Zararis except that there was no-one older and more responsible."

The way the Princess spoke made Lord Victor laugh again.

In fact he found himself laughing at almost everything she said.

She insisted on walking all round the deck and was like a child with a new toy.

Lord Victor realised that after living very simply in the country there was a fascination for her in everything she saw.

She asked him innumerable questions about the ship.

Finally he told her she would have to ask any more of the Captain because he had exhausted his knowledge of the subject.

"It is so much nicer for me that you are here," she said warmly, "because I was told there was an elderly man coming to represent Her Majesty who had escorted a number of other Princesses to be married and knew the protocol from A to Z."

This, as Lord Victor knew, was Lord Ludgate, for whom he had been substituted by the Queen.

When they went down to luncheon, he had begun to think that the voyage was going to be very different from what he had expected.

The Princess chattered away while they ate a well-cooked meal.

Listening to her, Lord Victor realised she had been extremely well educated.

"I had Governesses and Tutors," she said in answer to his question. "There were dozens of them, but what I enjoyed more than anything else was riding my Grandfather's horses. His sons insisted that he had the very best, and when they were home they would race me and challenge me to jump higher than they did."

Lord Victor thought that was something he would like to do himself.

However he decided it would be a mistake to say so.

He was aware before the luncheon was ended that if the Princess had been surprised that he had been appointed to escort her to Zararis, so were the Ladies-in-Waiting.

He was sure when the Princess was talking to him so spontaneously that they were watching and listening with disapproval.

When the luncheon ended one of the Baronesses said:

"I think, Your Royal Highness, you would be wise to rest after luncheon, otherwise you will find the journey unnecessarily tiring."

"Rest?" the Princess exclaimed. "I have no intention of doing that!"

"I think it is what you should do, Your Royal Highness," the other Baroness said in a repressive tone.

"Quite frankly, I want some exercise," the Princess insisted, "and I am hoping that Lord Victor will race me round the decks, or think of some other way I can tire myself out. Otherwise I shall want to stay up all night!"

Lord Victor saw the expression of horror on the elderly women's faces.

He realised the Princess was teasing them.

At the same time he understood that at eighteen she had no wish to lie down after luncheon.

"I suspect," he said, "that Her Royal Highness has never played Deck-Tennis. That is something I will teach her, and it will certainly provide some of the exercise she needs."

The two Baronesses sighed with relief, but the Ambassador said with a frown:

"Somebody should be in attendance upon Her Royal Highness."

There was such an expression of consternation on the faces of the Ladies-in-Waiting that Lord Victor said quickly:

"I will take care of Her Royal Highness, and I think we should agree from the beginning of this voyage that one person in attendance at a time is quite enough."

"Yes of course, Lord Victor," the Princess said,

"and do please all of you remember that I have never had all this attention in the past. I was allowed to ride alone all over my Grandfather's Estate, and I am finding all this molly-coddling somewhat of a bore."

The two Ladies-in-Waiting held up their hands in horror, but the Ambassador said:

"Of course Your Royal Highness must enjoy yourself while you can. You are well aware that once you reach Zararis, wherever you go and whatever you do, a Lady-in-Waiting must always be with you."

There was a little silence.

Then the Princess said:

"My Father used to say 'Never jump a fence until you come to it.' So, as Your Excellency suggests, I will enjoy myself to-day, and not worry for the moment about tomorrow."

Lord Victor could not help thinking she was being rather clever.

As he rose to his feet the Ambassador said to the Princess:

"There is one thing Your Royal Highness must not forget, and that is to learn the language that is spoken in Zararis while we have this free time on our hands."

"I have not forgotten," the Princess said, "and actually I do not think it will be difficult as it is basically Greek."

"That is what I heard," Lord Victor said, "and as I am anxious to learn the language myself, perhaps we could speak it while we are having meals."

"That is an excellent idea!" the Princess cried. "Anyway, I will teach you Greek."

"I know a little already," Lord Victor replied, "but I have not spoken it since I was at Oxford, and I am therefore what we might call 'somewhat rusty'."

"It will soon come back to you," the Princess said reassuringly, "and it is very lucky is it not, that having a Greek Father, I am to go to a country where the language is basically Greek. Her Majesty might have sent me to some place where they spoke only Chinese, or some other language of which I do not recognise a word!"

"I agree with Your Royal Highness," Lord Victor said, "and I shall be very grateful if, Ma'am, you will revive what I know of the Greek language."

He thought as he spoke and looked at her that Greek was the natural language for anyone so lovely.

He found it fascinating the way her eyes expressed eloquently every thought that was in her mind.

Her golden hair seemed to catch the rays of the sun which came through the port-holes.

"Now all that is decided," the Princess said, "so let us go on deck."

She deliberately spoke in Greek, but Lord Victor understood and followed her from the Cabin.

Only when they were outside did she whisper:

"Thank goodness we got away! I had an awful feeling that one of the 'Watch-dogs' would be sent with us."

Lord Victor was sure that he ought not to allow her to talk like that.

But as once again she made him laugh, there was nothing he could say.

He found as the afternoon progressed that she

quickly learnt the Tennis that was played on board ship.

They also walked round the deck a dozen times.

To give him practice she talked mostly in Greek, and Lord Victor found the language coming back to him.

It was one of the languages for which he had been specially commended when he was at Oxford.

In fact he had always found foreign languages easy.

He was sure that when he came to Zararis he would soon be able to understand ordinary people.

This of course was essential if he was to obtain the information which the Marquess of Salisbury wanted.

It was almost at the end of the afternoon when he suddenly had an idea.

The Princess had sat down on the windward side of the Battleship.

They were having their last glimpse of the coast of Britain.

"I suppose you know, Ma'am," Lord Victor said, "that the Russians have been causing a great deal of trouble in the Balkans?"

He expected her to look surprised, but instead she said:

"Yes, my Grandfather told me how they were trying to stir up trouble in a number of States, and warned me it was something I must try to counteract when I am Queen of Zararis."

"I have just thought," Lord Victor went on, "that it would be very helpful if you learnt Russian."

The Princess turned towards him eagerly.

"Do you know," she said, "I thought of that

myself, and actually I looked in Grandpapa's Library and found several books on Russian, which I have brought with me."

"That should be very useful," Lord Victor said. "And I will ask the Captain if there is anyone aboard who speaks that extremely difficult language."

Impulsively, as she did everything else, the Princess said:

"Let us go and ask him at once. Of course I should know Russian, otherwise all sorts of terrible things may be happening behind my back."

She did not wait for Lord Victor to agree, but set off towards the Bridge where they found the Captain.

The Princess explained what she wanted and the Captain said slowly:

"That is a sensible idea, Your Royal Highness, and I can tell you the Russians are everywhere! When we were in the Eastern Mediterranean last year, I bumped into them wherever I went, and I found it essential to have someone aboard who could speak their language."

"Is there anyone like that with you now?" the Princess enquired.

"There is, Ma'am, but I doubt if he speaks the sort of Russian you would find in their Palaces!"

Lord Victor did not say anything.

He was however aware that in the Winter Palace in St. Petersburg the Tsar and his family, like all the Russian nobility spoke French.

In fact it was a standing joke among the Diplomats.

Having taken the trouble to learn Russian before

they left home, they found they had to go into the Servants' quarters or into the streets to find anybody they could speak it to.

"I want to spend an hour or so every day learning Russian from the man you have on board," the Princess said positively.

"He will be very honoured, Ma'am," the Captain said, "but I am not sure if His Excellency will approve."

"I have given my approval," Lord Victor said, "for I am sure Her Majesty Queen Victoria, whom I represent, would think it an excellent idea. Her Royal Highness should be able to understand and converse in any language which is used in the country over which she is to rule."

He spoke rather pompously and the Captain said quickly:

"Yes, yes, of course, My Lord, I agree with you. I will send for Alexander, as he calls himself. But I rather fancy he has adopted the Tsar's name to make himself seem more important."

Later when they left the Bridge they found Alexander waiting for them.

He had obviously washed and made himself presentable.

A few questions told Lord Victor that the man was in fact half Russian.

He had been conceived when his English Father's ship had been in Port at Odessa.

Afterwards he was orphaned and brought up by some Missionaries in Russia.

At twenty he had gone to England where he joined the British Navy.

He was intelligent and used his knowledge of

Russian to bring him more money than he would otherwise have earned.

Lord Victor arranged that he and the Princess would take lessons from him every morning while they were at sea.

He asked if the stewards could turn one of the Cabins not being used into a Sitting-Room where they could learn in private.

The Captain promised to arrange this, and the Princess said approvingly:

"That was clever of you, My Lord. We do not want the 'Watch-dogs' sitting with us. I am certain they would disapprove of my speaking a language not their own, especially one they will not understand."

"I agree with you, Ma'am," Lord Victor said. "At the same time, I think it would be a mistake for us to upset your Ladies-in-Waiting."

"I try not to," the Princess expostulated, "but they gave me a long lecture this morning before breakfast which amounted to saying that I was not to be too familiar with you."

Lord Victor laughed.

"That is something I was afraid they might do," he said.

"They would be much happier," the Princess said, "if you had a long white beard and walked about on two sticks!"

"Then I must disappoint them," Lord Victor said, "because that is something that will not happen to me for a long time."

The Princess gave a little jump for joy.

"It is wonderful for me having you with me," she said. "I cannot imagine the old Gentleman who should have been in your place playing Deck-Tennis with me, or taking me down to the Engine-Room, where I intend to go now."

"Who said you could do that?" Lord Victor asked.

"The Captain," the Princess replied. "If you do not want to come, you can stay behind, but I think it will be very exciting!"

"I am sure, Ma'am, it will be very good for my education," Lord Victor said in an exaggeratedly humble tone.

The Princess laughed.

"What I would like to do," she said, "is to stop at all the countries we will be passing before we reach our destination. Then you and I could explore places like Tangier, Tunis, Malta and Crete. Think how exciting that would be!"

"It would indeed," Lord Victor replied, "but the Queen is anxious that we should reach Zararis as quickly as possible, so I fear there is little chance of our stopping anywhere on the way."

He was thinking as he spoke that it would have been very enjoyable.

He had to admit to himself that having been anxious in the first place to get the voyage over as quickly as possible and return home, he was now enjoying being with the Princess.

"It will not last," he told himself. "At the same time, she is certainly beautiful and different from any other woman I have ever met before."

She had a way with her that he had not expected in anyone so young.

When they went down to the Engine-Room she shook hands with the Chief Engineer Officer and talked to the others.

She was so charming as she did so that Lord Victor knew they were completely captivated by her.

Because she was so young she was unaware of her beauty and behaved naturally and unself-consciously.

He was used to women arranging themselves in seductive poses and moving with an artificial grace.

They thought out every move they made in order to attract the men who watched them.

But the Princess really enjoyed meeting the stokers in the Boiler-Room as much as she would have enjoyed talking with the Diplomats at Windsor Castle.

Or even, Lord Victor thought, his own contemporaries on a Ball-Room floor.

'One thing is quite certain,' he thought before he went to sleep that night, 'she will make an excellent Queen, and I only hope King Stephan is worthy of her.'

. . . .

The following day they started their lessons in Russian, and they spoke Greek at breakfast and luncheon.

After only one day of learning the game, the Princess beat Lord Victor at Deck-Tennis.

"I have won! I have won!" she claimed with the delight of a child.

"I must be getting old!" Lord Victor said.

"What you are is a very good teacher!" she answered. "Now we can really fight on equal terms!"

"And have a prize at the end of the game," he added. "I wonder what that will be?"

There was a little pause.

He knew that any other woman of his acquaintance would make it clear by the expression in her eyes what she would offer if she was defeated.

But the Princess merely smiled and said:

"I can think of something I could give you that would be really useful."

"What would that be, Ma'am?" Lord Victor enquired.

"There are so many presents one gets at Christmas and on Birthdays that are quite useless. Mama used to put them in a special drawer so that we could give them to the Bazaars for Charity, or to relatives we did not particularly like."

Lord Victor laughed.

"Is that what I am going to get?"

"I am not certain," the Princess said, "that it would not be easier to let you beat me. Then you would have to give me a present."

"In that case, you will have to tell me what you would like," Lord Victor said.

They were sitting in the sunshine as they were talking.

Now the Princess looked across the sea to the distant horizon.

Lord Victor was aware of how exquisite her profile was, and almost exactly like a statue of Venus which he remembered seeing in Rome.

Her hair had become a little loose whilst she had been so energetic and was lying against her cheeks.

Lord Victor thought that, if he touched it, it would be silky in his hands.

Then he told himself sharply that that was not

the way he should be thinking about the Princess.

"You have not answered my question," he said. "What would you like to have more than anything else?"

Slowly, in a soft voice, the Princess said:

"I first started to think . . two or three years ago . . that one day . . I would be married and . . I thought that like Papa and Mama . . I would . . fall very much . . in love."

"I suppose every young girl dreams that 'Prince Charming' will come into her life," Lord Victor said, "and they will marry and live happily ever after."

"That is . . what I . . thought would . . happen," the Princess said, "but now . . I have to marry a man I have . . never . . s.seen . . ."

Her voice died away.

Suddenly in a quite different tone she asked:

"What can I do if I hate him? Supposing I cannot bear to let him . . touch me?"

Lord Victor drew in his breath.

Seeing how young she was, it was something he had already thought of himself.

Now she was looking at him directly. Her eyes were very expressive and he saw the fear in them.

"I think you have to realise," he said quietly, "that as a Royal Personage you have to accept that your marriage, when it does take place, is a Political event and not an emotional one, as it is with ordinary people."

"I know that . . of course I know that!" the Princess said. "But I am frightened now when I . . think about it."

"Of course you are," Lord Victor agreed, "but

you have to remember that what is of first importance is the safety of thousands of people who will
suffer if their country is overrun by an enemy, and
the one person who can prevent that from happening
in Zararis is you!"

"I know that," Princess Sydella said. "As my
Grandfather explained, I am really only a Political
pawn. But I still breathe and feel like any other girl!"

"That is true," Lord Victor agreed. "At the same
time, you are a very special person, and that is why
you have to think in a different way from how you
have done before."

"I am trying to do that," the Princess said, "but I
cannot . . change the way I feel and . . I know that
what I really want . . and what perhaps I shall never
be allowed to have is . . Love."

Her voice was very soft and she almost whispered
the word.

Lord Victor was thinking despairingly that there
was absolutely nothing he could do to help her.

CHAPTER FOUR

The sea had subsided and the sun was shining brightly.

The roughness and turmoil of the Bay of Bişcay was almost forgotten.

Princess Sydella stretched out her legs in the place Lord Victor had found her on the windward side of the battleship.

"Do you think they would be very shocked," she asked, "if I took off my stockings?"

"Took off your stockings?" he repeated in a surprised voice. "Why should you want to do that?"

"I like the sun on my skin," she said, "and it is very hot here."

"I think your Ladies-in-Waiting would be extremely shocked at such an exposure," Lord Victor said, but his eyes were twinkling.

The Princess sighed.

"It is always the same when it is anything I want to do," she said. "It used to be 'a lady does not do that,' now it will be 'a Queen does not do that,' which will be even worse."

"I am sure it will," Lord Victor said sympathetically, "and certainly as a Queen you must not shock anybody."

"Do you like seeing people who are not wearing a lot of clothes?" Princess Sydella asked unexpectedly.

"What do you mean by that?" Lord Victor asked.

She did not answer immediately, but after a while said:

"Tell me, I am interested. It is what the Ladies-in-Waiting were saying when they thought I could not hear. They were saying you are very infatuated with a beautiful lady in Paris and when you went to see her she was only wearing a pearl necklace."

The Princess dropped her voice at the last words as if she too was rather shocked.

Lord Victor could not help smiling to himself.

He recalled the incident all too well although he could not imagine how it reached the aged Ladies-in-Waiting.

Then he remembered that some of his friends with him were members of White's.

If there was one place where the gossip went from mouth to mouth and ear to ear it was the White's Club in St. James Street.

What had happened just two months ago as Lord Victor told Queen Victoria, he had gone to Paris.

There had been six of them.

They went over especially for a party given by one of their friends who was celebrating his 40th birthday.

He had chosen what was usually a conventional family affair to go to Paris as a bachelor.

He had invited a number of his men friends to accompany him.

They knew more or less what to expect.

When they arrived in Paris they found their host

was giving a large dinner party in the house of one of the most famous *Cocottes* in the City.

The house was an extremely expensive one just off the *Champs Elysée*.

The female guests were all famous courtesans of the day.

They were all exquisitely dressed and Lord Victor thought somewhat wryly they would also be exceedingly expensive clothes.

It was obvious that the dinner itself was the very finest a French Chef could produce.

There was pâté and caviare which had been brought from Russia for the occasion to start with.

The truffles were the finest in France.

The drinks were all of an old vintage.

Lord Victor was not surprised to see on every lady's place at the table a delicately laundered table napkin.

Each one contained a note for 1000 francs.

It was amusing the way the notes disappeared almost as soon as they were discovered.

Yet undoubtedly they encouraged the conversation to be warmer and more amusing from the moment they were received.

It was a party that would have scandalised Queen Victoria.

But one which Lord Victor knew he would always remember.

Several of the women guests danced the can-can to amuse the men while they were still sitting at the table.

It was certainly an elaboration of the can-can as Lord Victor had seen it in Montmartre.

It would by the way it was performed have been banned in any public place.

It was received with noisy applause by the diners who embraced the dancers when it was finished.

They plied them with more champagne as they sat on their knees to drink it.

Lord Victor remembered getting back to where they were staying long after dawn had broken.

He had slept until luncheon the following day.

He thought that without exception it was one of the most amusing if slightly outrageous parties he had ever attended.

He did however remember that he had made an appointment for three o'clock that afternoon.

It was with the Charmer who had been sitting on his left-hand side.

She told him where her house was situated which was just off the Boire.

When he was dressed he felt more like himself.

He then thought it would be interesting to see if she was as beautiful in the daylight as she had seemed yesterday evening.

The majority of his friends who had come from London with him also had appointments.

They had every intention of keeping them.

He set off on his own to drive to Madame Mimi's house.

He timed it so that he would arrive at exactly the time he had promised her he would call.

The house was small but from what he had heard last night, Madame Mimi could choose from among her protectors the richest men in Paris.

When the door was opened by a very smartly

dressed maid he could see that the furniture was antique and in excellent taste.

The pictures on the wall all worthy of being in the Louvre.

His top hat and his cane were taken from him and he was escorted up an attractive staircase to the first floor.

The maid paused at a door of a room which Lord Victor thought would open on to a garden at the back.

When the maid stood aside he entered the room and heard the door close behind him.

For a moment he thought the room was empty.

Then at the far end in the sunshine coming through the window he saw Madame Mimi was waiting for him.

She was standing poised against a magnificent arrangement of yellow orchids which must have cost a fortune.

It was a background for her dark hair, huge dark eyes and most of all for the whiteness of her skin.

She was waiting for him and wearing only one thing around her long neck, a perfect pearl necklace.

As it flashed through Lord Victor's mind he realised that Princess Sydella was waiting for his answer.

Choosing his words carefully, he said:

"I admire beauty wherever I find it and beautiful women are invariably a joy to behold."

"I cannot understand," the Princess replied, "why the lady was wearing only a necklace."

"You know as well as I do," Lord Victor said, "the conversation was not meant for your ears and let me say once and for all the ladies that you have heard about in Paris would not be accepted in your Mother's Drawing-Room and certainly not in yours when you are the Queen."

"What I find difficult to understand," the Princess retorted somewhat petulantly, "is that they can do all sorts of extraordinary things while you say it would shock people on board this ship if I just took off my stockings."

There was something very childlike in the way she was arguing.

Lord Victor thought for the thousandth time how difficult it would be for her in the future.

How would she cope with the protocol and pomp which was inevitable in any Palace however small.

Aloud he said:

"What Your Royal Highness has to do is to enjoy yourself as much as you can. You will be living in a very different world to the one you know already so you have to accept what occurs and try not to let it upset you or in any way shock you."

"I cannot believe I shall be shocked," the Princess said, "and I am much more likely to die of boredom than anything else."

"Now that is being very pessimistic," Lord Victor said. "I am sure there will be many things to interest you that you have never seen before.

"There will be unusual people and I hope intelligent ones who will explain to you how you can help the country and of course the King."

There was silence and then she said:

"Suppose the King . . prefers ladies . . like you . . visited in Paris and . . finds me very . . dull?"

"I am sure that would be impossible," Lord

Victor said. "No-one could possibly call Your Royal Highness dull."

"Well that is one point in my favour," the Princess said. "But . . suppose . . *I* find *him* . . very dull?"

She spoke in a low voice as if she was frightened of being overheard.

Lord Victor thought this was extremely likely.

There was nothing he could say, but thought the best thing was to change the subject.

The Princess was so intrigued by what she had heard had happened in Paris.

Before he could think of a subject they could discuss without embarrassment, she said:

"Did you love the lady who was wearing only pearls around her neck?"

"That is a question you must not ask me," Lord Victor said.

"Why not!" the Princess enquired.

"Because that concerns my private life.

"Also as I have already explained the ladies at that particular party would never be accepted by your Mother. And more certainly would never be referred to by Queen Victoria. In fact if their names were mentioned at Windsor Castle everyone would pretend they did not exist."

"They . . existed to . . you," the Princess insisted.

"That is different," Lord Victor replied.

"Why is it different?"

"Because I am a man."

"So men are allowed to meet strange ladies wearing no clothes," the Princess said, "while women must just pretend they are not there."

"Now you have got it exactly right," Lord Victor said. "You must understand Your Royal Highness that at this moment we cannot discuss the subject any further."

"If I cannot discuss it with you, or with anyone else, how am I going to learn about such things," the Princess asked.

"There are many other things for you to be interested in," Lord Victor said, "that are not so improper for a Princess."

"Do you think I could persuade the King when I am married to him to take me to Paris?"

"If you went to Paris you would find it very dull," Lord Victor said. "You would very likely be staying at your own Embassy and you would be allowed to dine at the British Embassy, the French Embassy and the Italian Embassy, but Montmartre and doubtless more amusing theatres would be banned to you although you might be allowed to go to the Opera."

"It is not fair," the Princess retorted.

"I think actually you will enjoy life in different ways without coming in contact with people who could mean absolutely nothing in your world or you in theirs."

It was difficult, Lord Victor thought, to try to explain to this child who was so innocent, the amusement of Paris for a man.

It would in fact never be tolerated by any of his womenfolk.

He thought it was typical of the old women to talk about it in front of the Princess.

If they heard such things as he supposed was inevitable, the least they could do was to keep their mouths shut.

"Now let us talk about something more interesting," he said.

"But I am interested in you," the Princess protested. "I want to know what sort of women you think attractive and why you have never married anyone?"

Lord Victor thought he could answer the second question quite easily.

He did not have enough money to get married.

Also he had not yet met anyone with whom he wished to spend the rest of his life.

Almost as if she read his thoughts, the Princess said:

"You must have been in love or were the women you met just in love with you?"

Lord Victor thought the conversation was far too intricate.

Yet he did not see how he could stop it without being unkind.

He therefore replied:

"I hope I shall get married one day. But I shall not marry unless I fall very much in love."

The Princess gave a little cry.

"So you were not in love with the woman wearing only a pearl necklace?"

Lord Victor thought he had fallen into that trap.

It was difficult to explain to this impulsive child that he had in fact hardly given a thought to Mimi after he left her.

If he went to Paris again he would not make any effort to call on her.

She was very experienced in every action which would attract and inflame a man.

It was all somehow artificial and he frankly was not interested.

It was easier to remember Nancy Weldon who

was responsible for him being in this ship with the Princess.

"You are thinking of someone very nice," the Princess said suddenly.

Lord Victor looked at her in astonishment.

"How could you possibly know that?"

"I was watching your eyes," she said. "When you are interested in something that is said, they are alert, but when you are thinking of something nice, they are softer and kinder."

"Now you do surprise me," Lord Victor said. "What do you think I should see in your eyes?"

The Princess laughed.

"Curiosity," she said. "I am curious about you because I have never met anyone like you before."

"But you must have met a great number of men who stayed with your Grandfather and of course with your Father and Mother."

"Papa's friends were the nicer," Princess Sydella answered. "Grandpapa's were rather old and pompous. They talked to me as if I was a small child to whom they would like to give some sweets."

"Now I think you are being rather critical," Lord Victor said.

"Papa taught me to be that," the Princess answered. "He said when you meet people do not take them just at their face value. Look deeply into them to see what they are really thinking. Sum them up so that you are never deceived by those who put on an act simply to impress you."

"That is very good advice," Lord Victor said approvingly. "I am sure that is what you will do when you are on the throne."

"When I am on the throne," the Princess replied,

"it will not be the same as sitting here talking to you."

That was true and he could not deny it.

After a silence he said:

"You will have the advantage of meeting a very varied collection of people you would not meet if you remained at home or became a *débutante*."

"There is no likelihood of that," the Princess said. "I think I would have stayed buried in the country if Queen Victoria had not sent for me."

"You ought to be very grateful," Lord Victor remarked.

"I am in a way, but at the same time I am . . frightened."

Lord Victor thought quickly this was dangerous ground.

"Do not think about it," he said, "forget tomorrow and concentrate about enjoying yourself today."

"That is what I am doing with you," the Princess said. "It is so exciting to have someone young and interesting on board with me instead of having to listen to those old women telling me what I should and should not do. The Ambassador continually talking about Zararis as if it was something he was selling me cheap off a barrow."

Lord Victor could not help laughing.

"You do say the most extraordinary things," he said, "especially for a young woman who tells me she has been brought up quietly in the country seeing no-one."

"I have seen the people on the Estate, and of course the horses," the Princess replied. "And when I talk to them I am sure they understand everything I say and would tell me very exciting things if they could talk."

"I have often thought that myself," Lord Victor agreed. "At the same time I have heard strange stories from people who I never thought had done anything in their lives but just plod along. I have been bored by brilliant people who I expected would thrill me, but who did the exact opposite."

The Princess laughed and it was a very pretty sound.

"It is wonderful being able to talk to you," she said. "Tell me more about yourself and why you were sent to escort me to Zararis instead of the old Statesman I was expecting?"

Lord Victor knew that was something he could not possibly tell the Princess.

After a moment he said:

"I think Queen Victoria who is my Godmother was being kind to me and also the Prime Minister the Marquess of Salisbury who thought I might be useful."

"Useful?" the Princess enquired.

"Finding out what exactly happened in Zararis with regard to the Russians who are all over the Balkans. They are only kept under control because they are afraid of Great Britain."

"Do you think we should be afraid of what they might do in Zararis before we get there?"

"I hope they will do nothing," Lord Victor said. "But at the same time it will be wise as we are British to keep our eyes and ears open. If we see anything which you think odd or if you hear anything which might be dangerous you must tell me immediately."

"Of course I will," the Princess said. "When

you have left me and gone home, what should I do then?"

It was a very sensible question and Lord Victor thought before he replied.

"I will look around when we arrive and see if there is anyone I can trust."

"It would be easier if you stayed yourself," the Princess suggested.

"That sounds very pleasant," Lord Victor said, "but I have things to do at home in England."

"With lovely ladies?"

Now they were back where they began and he said:

"That is a question you must not ask me. It is definitely indiscreet."

"Why? I am very interested. As soon as I saw you I thought you were not only handsome and young which is such a change from the other men, but also I could trust you."

"That is a very nice thing to say," Lord Victor answered, "and I am very flattered. I hope you will always trust me. But at the same time I promise to try and find you someone you can trust in the same way when I have left."

"Suppose you do not find anyone," the Princess queried.

"There must be lots of men in Zararis," Lord Victor answered. "They cannot all be old and decrepit or slightly crooked."

"I suppose not," the Princess agreed, "but I just wish this voyage could go on and on and we could go all round the world and back again before we stop."

"That is something people have wished since the beginning of time," Lord Victor said, "but it is only very occasionally they find it possible to reach the horizon and find there is another horizon ahead and so on without giving up the chase."

The Princess did not speak and as if he wished to elaborate his theme he said:

"It is the same when anyone climbs a mountain only to find there is another mountain beyond it and another beyond that."

He then went on:

"Very few people achieve what they set out to find in the world. It is the effort that counts and an effort that we all have to make."

He thought as he spoke that it was something he had not worked out for himself before now.

It was the Princess who had made him think differently to the way he had thought in the past.

He looked at her.

When she was looking serious she was even lovelier than when she was laughing.

'How can anything so exquisite be wasted on an old man who would not appreciate her' he asked himself almost angrily.

Then he was determined not to be personally involved in this drama.

He had been unwillingly pushed into what could only be a passing interlude in his life.

He was well aware that if he became too involved with the Princess it would be hard to get away.

It would be difficult to leave her to the people who did not understand her and with whom he could see she had very little in common.

'She is so lovely, so unspoilt and so innocent' he thought.

She should not be involved in what will undoubtedly bring her nothing but disappointment and distress.

Then a thought flashed through his mind and he felt he must be mad.

Here he was pitying and worrying over a young woman of no particular importance who was going to be crowned Queen.

Although she would rule over a very small country it was important in British eyes.

A great number of other people would also think it important.

He should be congratulating her and telling her how lucky she was.

That was what the great majority of people in England would do if they were in his place.

Yet he knew if he faced the truth the Princess Sydella would be like a bird caught in a cage from which she could never escape.

People could stare at her and admire her but she could never spread her wings.

Never fly high into the sky and never have any real freedom.

'It is wrong and against nature,' Lord Victor told himself.

Then he heard Princess Sydella's soft voice asking:

"Why are you looking . . angry . . what have I . . said to . . upset you?"

"It is nothing you have said," Lord Victor said quickly. "It is something I was thinking about of which I disapproved."

"Was it because I am being sent to Zararis to . . marry the . . King?"

'She is too perceptive,' he thought, 'and at the same time too sensitive.'

He knew that what was lying ahead of her was something entirely alien to her character and to her personality.

There was nothing he could do about it, absolutely nothing.

Except just watch the prison walls close on something small and exquisite, which ought to be in the sunshine.

When they went down below they found there was no-one in their cabin.

When tea was brought by the steward the Princess poured it out.

They talked of other things than those which had concerned them on deck until they were joined by the Ambassador.

He too had spent most of the time in the Bay of Biscay in his cabin.

It had only been the Princess and Lord Victor who had braved the elements.

They laughed as the waves soaked them as they tried to walk precariously round the deck.

"The worst is over," the Ambassador said without much elation in his voice. "From now on it will be calmer and there is no need for anyone to be sea-sick."

He was obviously speaking for himself.

Lord Victor had the suspicion that he had been prostrate like the Ladies-in-Waiting while it had been so rough.

He had always been a good sailor and the Princess had been delighted to find that she was one.

"Papa always said women were a nuisance at sea

78

because they were sick and made a fuss about it. I was not sick and did not make a fuss, did I?" she asked.

"You were splendid," Lord Victor said.

He spoke quite casually and saw her eyes light up.

He told himself he must be very careful not to make her too interested in him.

She must not depend on him so that it would be even harder for her when he left.

Because the Ambassador settled down in the cabin and obviously had no intention of leaving, the Princess said:

"I must have a breath of fresh air before it gets dark, please Lord Victor come with me."

He thought it was a mistake but without seeming rude, there was nothing he could do but accept.

He helped the Princess into her coat she had been wearing before.

As they went up the companionway he said:

"I think perhaps we are being rather rude in leaving the Ambassador alone."

"If we stay he will only lecture me more than he has already today and if anything would put me off Zararis, it is hearing about it for hours on end."

"I sympathize with you," Lord Victor said, "but at the same time the more you can learn about it the better. As I have already said, we both have to be on our guard."

"It will be fun doing that with you," the Princess said pointedly.

She moved a little closer to him as he spoke.

He had the feeling that she wanted to hold his hand.

Quickly he thrust his in his pocket saying:

"Be careful you do not slip on the wet deck. Are you quite certain you are warm enough?"

"Quite certain," the Princess answered. "But I think it is very kind of you to think of me and to be concerned in case I catch a chill."

"I cannot allow you to arrive coughing and spitting," Lord Victor said.

The Princess laughed.

"That will certainly be very unromantic."

She spoke without thinking and then her expression changed and she said:

"There will be nothing very romantic anyway, about my wedding to the King, will there?"

"You cannot say that until you have met His Majesty," Lord Victor replied. "After all he sounds old to you but some men are still young at that age."

There was silence and then he said:

"Surely they brought you a portrait or a miniature of the King?"

"I did ask if I could see one," the Princess replied, "but they told me he had always refused to be painted. So perhaps he is very ugly or there is something wrong with him."

"Now you are just being imaginative," Lord Victor said hastily.

At the same time he thought it ridiculous that everything was so badly organised.

Surely if they were prepared to bring out a girl of eighteen to marry a man of sixty-five they should try to get him to sound somewhat attractive for her.

The Princess was walking along with her head bent.

"What do you think would happen," she said, "if

at the last moment I said 'No, I will not marry the King and I want to go home'?"

"You could not do anything like that," Lord Victor said hastily. "You will not only be letting down yourself and your family, but the Queen and the whole British Empire."

He thought she would take this seriously, but to his surprise she laughed.

"Now you are making me out to be very important which is something I have not felt despite all the curtseying and bowing I have received."

"Just remember you are important," Lord Victor said. "You cannot do anything outrageous which will have the whole Empire screaming at you, and perhaps end up being imprisoned in the Tower of London."

He was speaking lightly and she laughed again.

"That would certainly cause a commotion and I am sure those dear old Yeomen would be very kind to me. At least I would be nearer home than if I was in Zararis."

"You must not think like that," Lord Victor said. "You must concentrate on the fact that you have been asked, and it is a great compliment, to sit on the throne of a country that is important to the balance of power."

The Princess held up her hand.

"Now please do not start," she said. "I have heard all this over and over again. I know that what I have to do is more or less to keep the peace in the world, instead I just want to be me."

She paused for a moment and then said in a different voice:

"I wish that instead of travelling on and on to

what is awaiting me at this tiresome Battleship, that you and I were galloping on Grandpapa's horses over the fields in England."

"I would like that too," Lord Victor said. "But it cannot happen and it is no use thinking about it."

"It is easy for you to say that, because you have just got to deposit me on the counter so to speak. Then you can go back to your friends and your lovely ladies and all the things you really enjoy."

"I know, I know," Lord Victor said. "It is very hard for you. But life is never the bed of roses they pretend it is, although surprising things happen when we least expect them."

"What else could happen to me?" Princess Sydella asked. "I was surprised when they told me I had to marry the King of Zararis. The only surprise now would be if he suddenly changed into a young man or when we arrive we find the Palace has been blown up and the Russians have taken over."

"You are not to talk like that," Lord Victor said almost angrily, "it is unlucky and also wrong that you should be thinking about these things instead of the good that you can do for the people who need you and want you."

He spoke sternly because he was worried by the way she was thinking.

When she turned away from him he thought he had been rather cruel.

They reached a sheltered part of the deck.

The Princess was standing protected from the wind and the waves with her back to Lord Victor.

He had a strange feeling that she was fighting against her tears.

He said quickly:

"Forgive me, I should not have spoken to Your Royal Highness like that, but I was really worrying about you in case some of your ridiculous ideas came true."

"You were . . worrying . . about me?"

"Of course I am," he answered. "You are so young and I realise that they are asking almost the impossible for someone who is quite unprepared for what lies ahead."

His voice softened as he went on:

"Because you are very courageous and at the same time very conscious of what other people feel, I know that when we reach Zararis you will be a great success and the people will love you."

"How can you be . . sure of . . that?" the Princess murmured.

"I think both you and I have feelings that we cannot explain but we know the truth," Lord Victor replied. "You know that what I am telling you is something to which you respond because it is good and because it is right. Tell me that is true."

"I . . will . . try," Princess Sydella said.

She turned round suddenly.

Lord Victor could see there were tears in her eyes and one had even run down her cheek.

"Please . . help me," she pleaded. "There is no-one else who . . understands except . . you, I am so . . very much . . alone."

"Of course I will help you," Lord Victor said. "Trust me and forgive me for what I have just said."

He put out his hands without thinking and took both of hers.

For a moment he just held them and then he bent his head and kissed one hand and then the other.

"You will succeed," he said very quietly, "I am sure of it."

CHAPTER FIVE

Alexander rose from the table at which they had been working.

He bowed to the Princess, then to Lord Victor.

"Ver' good!" he said. "Ver' good today. Am honoured an' proud you do so well."

He then left the cabin and Lord Victor said:

"He is right. Do you realise that in just over ten days we really have progressed a long way in this appallingly difficult language?"

"That is true," the Princess said. "But I do not like Alexander. He has hard eyes."

Lord Victor smiled and almost without thinking said:

"While your eyes are soft and very beautiful!"

The Princess looked surprised at the compliment, but he went on as if he was talking to himself:

"If we could stop at Athens, I would take you to the Acropolis and compare you to a Greek goddess!"

"I would love that," the Princess said.

"But as it is impossible," Lord Victor went on in a rather hard voice, "we must just get on with our lessons until we arrive in Zararis."

He made a movement as if he would go towards the door.

The Princess was still standing at the table.

She was looking down at the notes she had made while Alexander was teaching them.

Softly she said in a low voice:

"It has been such . . fun because we are . . doing this . . together. It will be very . . different when I am . . a Queen, and I have a feeling . . that the . . only people I will have to . . talk to will be like . . Mr. Orestes."

Mr. Orestes was the Statesman representing the Prime Minister of Zararis, who had been exceedingly boring at breakfast on the first day.

Once however the sea began to get rough, he had disappeared from sight, like the two Ladies-in-Waiting.

All three of them had remained in their cabins until the ship had passed through the Bay of Biscay.

The sea had in fact been very turbulent.

At the same time the sun was shining, and the Princess had enjoyed watching the waves.

When they broke over the bow of the ship she clapped her hands and laughed.

She and Lord Victor had only been able to snatch a little exercise when it was momentarily calmer.

When they reached the Mediterranean, the two Baronesses reappeared.

They looked white and shaken, and said they had suffered from severe sea-sickness all the time they had been absent.

Mr. Orestes on reappearing had not admitted to being ill.

He merely announced that he had been working on a report he was making on Princess Sydella's Royal blood.

When he told them this the Princess said:

"I am very flattered that you should take so much trouble, Mr. Orestes, but is it really so important?"

"Very important indeed, Your Royal Highness!" he replied in a serious tone. "The people of Zararis will wish to know exactly how close is your connection with Her Majesty Queen Victoria."

He made the last words sound like a trumpet-call.

Lord Victor could not refrain from saying:

"You will find a great number of people in England have traces of Royal blood in their family tree. I, for instance, can claim a relationship to King Charles II, but only through a woman called Nell Gwyn, who started life by selling oranges at the Drury Lane Theatre in London."

The Princess laughed and said:

"I must send you an orange as a birthday present."

Mr. Orestes however seemed interested.

"Is what you have just said really true?" he asked.

"It is quite true," Lord Victor declared. "King Charles made the son he had by Nell Gwyn the Duke of St. Albans, and my Mother is the aunt of his descendant, the present Duke."

"Then of course," the Princess chimed in, "because you are also a Godson of the Queen, Her Majesty will have to find a throne for you."

Lord Victor held up his hands in horror.

"I hope not," he said. "I wish to enjoy myself, and I can assure Mr. Orestes that no-one in England is the slightest bit interested in my few drops of Royal blood!"

Mr. Orestes however was making notes.

Only when they left the cabin did the Princess say:

"Was it true what you told him? He will now

spend hours in trying to trace you back to King Charles!"

"Let him!" Lord Victor said lightly. "I assure you, there are quite a number of people can claim the doubtful distinction of being born on what is called 'the wrong side of the blanket'!"

After that they had gone to the cabin where Alexander was waiting for them.

Now the Princess said:

"I have enjoyed learning Russian, but it will all be a waste of time if there is no-one to talk to."

"According to the Marquess of Salisbury," Lord Victor answered, "the Russians are everywhere, but if you are looking for a tall, dark, handsome Prince, you will have to go to Russia."

"I would rather talk Russian with . . you," the Princess replied.

Lord Victor thought that was what he would like himself.

Then he knew that he must be very careful.

He was well aware that because they were together all day, the Princess talked to him quite spontaneously and intimately.

It was something that must cease as soon as they arrived at their destination.

He also had the uncomfortable feeling that she was a little in love with him.

Yet, because she was so young and innocent, she was unaware of it.

He admitted to himself when he was in the darkness of his cabin that he found her fascinating.

He had never in his whole life spent so much time alone with a young woman.

Instead of counting the hours, as he had expected

to do, until he could escape, he found her more and more interesting, day by day.

It was not only because she was so beautiful.

Every movement she made had a grace that was natural and of which she was unself-conscious.

It was not only because her features were classically perfect.

The expressions on her face which succeeded one another were, he thought, each more entrancing than the last.

But there was something else and quite different.

Something he had never encountered before and of which, he told himself, he was afraid.

It was the undeniable affinity between them!

They laughed at the same jokes and seemed able to read each other's thoughts.

Lord Victor had never found this with the women to whom he had made love.

In some strange way he could not explain, he was closer to the Princess than to any woman he had ever known.

He was intelligent enough to realise that it was because their minds had become each a part of the other's.

It was therefore more subtle than if it had been their bodies.

"Whatever happens," Lord Victor had been telling himself every night, "I must not let her fall in love with me, so that she is unhappy when I leave."

He watched the sunshine coming through the port-hole.

It turned her hair into a golden halo round her head.

He was asking himself as he did so whether he

would be happy when he left Zararis on H.M.S. *Victorious*, and returned to England alone.

Suddenly, as if she did not wish to continue what she was thinking, the Princess pushed the papers on the table to one side and said:

"The sun is shining and we have time for a run round the deck before luncheon. But hurry! hurry! before one of the 'Watch-dogs' tries to stop us!"

There was no-one to do so.

Lord Victor knew perceptively that she was thinking that in a day or so it would no longer be possible for her to run round the deck.

She would be surrounded by all the pomp and ceremony that was waiting for her in the country over which she was to reign.

That evening at dinner, rather unwisely, Lord Victor thought, the Ambassador said:

"We are not very far from Athens now. I have always thought the lights of the City in the darkness with the stars overhead, is one of the most beautiful sights in the world!"

The Princess jumped up from the table.

"We must go and see it!" she exclaimed.

"It is too early," Lord Victor replied, "the last rays of the sun are still on the horizon."

"Then that will be beautiful too!" the Princess replied. "How could Greece be anything but beautiful, whatever time of the day it is?"

She had reached the cabin door as she spoke.

As they heard her running towards the companionway no-one moved.

Lord Victor was therefore obliged to follow her.

He found her on deck.

The horizon was tinged with the crimson of the sunset.

It looked, he had to admit, like something out of a Fairy Tale.

"It is lovely! Lovely!" the Princess said in a rapt little voice. "I can understand how Papa often felt homesick for his own country, even though he was so happy with Mama."

Because Lord Victor was afraid of the emotion in her voice he asked:

"I have often wondered why your Mother has not come with you to be present at your marriage and your Coronation."

"She wanted to . . of course she wanted to," Princess Sydella replied, "but she suffered from acute rheumatism last Winter and it is still impossible for her to walk up and down stairs."

Her voice was sad as she went on:

"Poor Mama has to be carried, except when she walks very, very slowly with two sticks on the Ground Floor. As she said herself, it would be very undignified to have to be carried by sailors up and down a Battleship!"

"I am sorry to hear that she is suffering," Lord Victor said, "but perhaps with the warmer weather, she will soon be better."

"I am praying that she will," the Princess answered, "but I am so very lucky to have you, otherwise those old fuddy-duddies would never let me do anything!"

She leaned over the ship's rail as she spoke and looked down at the sea.

"Perhaps we will see a dolphin," she said. "Like those which were sacred to Apollo."

"I think," Lord Victor replied, pointing with his left hand, "that Delphi must be somewhere over there and it is a place I have always wanted to visit."

"Oh, do let us go there together!" the Princess pleaded. "I would love to stand beneath the 'Shining Cliffs' with you. And I am sure, although the Temples are in ruins and the statues stolen, we shall be able to visualise it in all its glory."

It struck Lord Victor that he would like to be there with the Princess.

Delphi had appealed to him ever since he first read about it.

Then he thought he was treading on dangerous ground and he said quickly:

"Have you any idea where your Father's island was? Perhaps we shall pass it before it gets too dark."

The Princess did not answer.

He saw that she was still looking at the sunset.

She was so very lovely in the fading light.

Lord Victor could see that the first evening star was just coming out overhead.

He had an overwhelming desire to put his arms around her.

He wanted to tell her that he would protect her from anything that would hurt or make her unhappy in the future.

Then hand-in-hand they would go to Delphi and become part of its magic which would never die.

He did not move or speak, but the Princess said in a rapt little voice:

"I am sure that Delphi would seem . . real to me . . as if I was a part of it . . perhaps we both were . . many years ago . ."

Lord Victor felt as if he was in a dream from which he had no wish to wake.

Then because he was afraid of his own feelings, he walked away to stand at the stern of the ship.

He looked with unseeing eyes at the crimson of the setting sun reflected on the smooth surface of the sea.

Then the Princess was beside him and she slipped her hand into his.

"Why did you move away?" she asked. "You are not . . angry with me?"

"No, of course not," he answered.

"Have I said . . something to . . upset you? If you do not tell me what is . . wrong I shall lie . . awake all night . . worrying."

"There is nothing wrong," Lord Victor replied.

He looked at her, saw the pleading expression in her eyes and said somewhat roughly:

"There is nothing wrong except that you are too lovely for any man's peace of mind."

He saw the expression of astonishment in her eyes.

Then as she realised that what he had said was a compliment, it was replaced by what he could only describe to himself as a rapture.

It was then he turned and walked away, leaving her alone.

Only when he reached his cabin did he admit to himself that he was in love.

He wondered what the hell he should do about it.

. . . .

The next day they were moving through the Northerly group of Greek islands.

Only as they passed up the Aegean Sea did the

Ambassador at luncheon tell them what lay ahead.

"I have not bothered Your Royal Highness with it before," he said, "but I think before we actually arrive at the Port of Zararis I should tell you what will happen."

"What will happen?" the Princess asked.

Lord Victor knew that she was suddenly nervous.

He also wondered what the Ambassador was about to explain.

There had been no mention until now of what was planned for their arrival.

He had thought to himself it would be the inevitable drive through the City with cheering crowds.

Then there would be long and exceedingly boring speeches by the Prime Minister and other dignitaries.

After that would be another Reception.

This would be when they reached the Palace, where presumably the King would be waiting to greet his future Bride.

Because he was an elderly man he would not hurry to greet Princess Sydella on the Battleship, as a younger man would have done.

Whatever happened, Lord Victor was quite certain it would all be extremely boring, both for the Princess and for himself.

There was only one redeeming feature of the ceremony.

That was they would understand what was being said in a language which from that moment on would be the Princess's.

She had asked him only yesterday if he thought there would be any English people in the Palace.

"I think that is unlikely," he replied, "although of

course there will be a British Embassy or Consulate in the City itself."

"Then suppose," Princess Sydella suggested, "I forget how to talk in English . . and have to start learning the language all over again when I . . go back to England to visit . . my Mother?"

Lord Victor tried to laugh.

"You are making unnecessary difficulties," he said, "and of course you will remember how to speak English! How could you possibly forget it? If I am not mistaken, you say your prayers in that language."

"I do, of course," the Princess said with a note of relief in her voice. "But can you imagine talking Greek, with all those funny words put in, day after day, year after year?"

She sighed before she added:

"And you must know that my jokes will not sound half so funny in Zararis."

Lord Victor knew this was true.

But he tried to help the Princess accept the inevitable.

"I am sure you will be able to ask some of your friends to come and stay with you! That would easily be possible, if you pay for those who cannot afford it."

"I never thought of that," the Princess exclaimed, her eyes lighting up, "and . . will you come and stay if I . . ask you?"

Feeling as he did at the moment, Lord Victor thought that would be a grave error.

But to make her happy he answered:

"Of course, I should be very honoured to have an invitation from the Queen of Zararis! At the same time, I will want to bring with me, if I do not have a wife, several of my horses."

The Princess gave a little cry.

"That would be wonderful! I promise you, here and now, that I will send a special Battleship – if we have one – to collect you and your horses."

She paused for a moment.

Then, as if she could not help herself, she asked:

"Is . . there anyone . . particular whom . . you want to . . marry?"

Lord Victor was sure this was an idea that had never occurred to her before, and she was hurt by the thought of it.

"I am a confirmed bachelor," he said quickly, "and I think it is unlikely I shall ever marry."

He was aware as he spoke that the sunshine had come back into her eyes, and she smiled.

It was then he told himself that he must not allow this sort of conversation to happen.

Nevertheless he was aware that it had.

"Now what has been planned," the Ambassador was saying in his slow, rather dreary voice, "is that as we near the Port of Zararis, a special Royal Barge will come out to collect Her Royal Highness, and those in attendance upon her."

Lord Victor was listening in surprise as the Ambassador went on:

"Her Royal Highness will sit on a throne made of flowers in the centre of the Barge, and an Orchestra will play behind her."

The Princess gave a little exclamation.

Lord Victor knew she was wondering if she would be allowed to dance.

"You will sit in state, Ma'am," the Ambassador

went on, "as the Barge moves down through lines of small boats, all decorated and specially lit."

"Why does this have to be at night?" Lord Victor enquired.

"Because, My Lord, everyone in the City and in the countryside will want to be there, and it would be impossible for every factory and shop to close their doors in the daytime."

Lord Victor nodded to show he understood, and the Ambassador went on:

"The illuminations on the road from the Quay to the Palace will make it as bright as daylight. Her Royal Highness will drive in an open carriage, so that everyone can see her."

His voice was almost dramatic as he said:

"When Her Royal Highness reaches the Palace, His Majesty will be waiting at the top of the steps to greet her."

Lord Victor was aware of the apprehension in Princess Sydella's eyes as he spoke the last words.

"I am sure Your Excellency has arranged it admirably!" he said quickly.

"You must thank the Prime Minister for that," the Ambassador said. "It was his idea, and we felt it would be a delightful entry into the City. The onlookers will undoubtedly take Her Royal Highness to their hearts."

"There will be flowers everywhere," one of the Baronesses said. "They will be arranged around the trees lining the route, and the children will throw them into the carriage."

"Your Royal Highness will be presented with a wreath of flowers to wear on your head," the other Baroness chimed in, "rather than a tiara."

Lord Victor thought this was an original idea.

At the same time, he knew without her saying so that the Princess was wondering where he would be.

"Lord Victor, representing Queen Victoria," the Ambassador answered, "will sit opposite Your Royal Highness with his back to the horses. The next carriage will contain your Ladies-in-Waiting and myself."

There was a note of satisfaction in his voice as he said the words.

"After that will come the Prime Minister and Members of the Council."

"What .. happens when we .. reach the .. Palace?" the Princess asked in a low voice.

"His Majesty will greet you and there will be a State Banquet at which we will all be present," the Ambassador answered.

He was waiting, Lord Victor knew, for some sign of appreciation from the Princess.

As she did not speak, he said:

"I see it has all been very well thought out. It will certainly be an original way of being greeted in a new country. I am sure other countries will copy such ceremonial in the future."

The Ambassador swelled with pride.

But the Princess said nothing until she was alone with Lord Victor.

They were going to play Deck-Tennis.

The two Baronesses had quickly made excuses so that they could lie down.

As they reached the deck, the Princess asked:

"Do I have .. to do all .. that?"

Lord Victor did not pretend to misunderstand the question and he replied:

"I think it is an excellent idea for the people over whom you will rule to see Your Royal Highness looking very lovely and surrounded by flowers, which, in my opinion, are far more becoming than jewels."

The Princess did not speak and after a moment he said:

"They are really doing their best, and it will be up to Your Royal Highness in the future to make all ceremonial more interesting and less tedious than it seems at the moment."

"You . . you think I can . . do that?" she asked hesitatingly.

"Of course you can!" Lord Victor said. "You have made this voyage, which I thought would be a long-drawn-out bore, enjoyable and entertaining for me. That is what you have to do in the future for a whole country!"

"But . . it has been enjoyable and . . entertaining for me," the Princess said, "because you are here."

"You did not know that before I came aboard," Lord Victor said, "and I am quite certain, even if it had been the old man whom you were expecting, he would have been entranced. It would have meant a new lease of life for him because you make everything you do, think and say what you call 'fun'."

There was silence. Then the Princess asked:

"Can I . . really do . . it?"

It was the question of a child who felt that everything was too big for her.

"Of course you can!" Lord Victor reassured her. "Try not to be frightened. Tell yourself that, if nothing else, you will make those over whom you rule laugh and discover the beautiful things in life, rather than those which are ugly."

"You are so sensible and so . . wise," Princess Sydella said, "and I want . . you to be . . there to tell me . . what to . . do."

There was a little pause.

Then Lord Victor said:

"You know that is impossible."

He walked towards the Deck-Tennis net that was waiting for them.

"Now I am going to beat you," he said, "unless you really exert yourself."

For a moment he thought the Princess was going to refuse to play.

Then, in a voice he could hardly hear, she said:

"That will be 'Love-All'!"

CHAPTER SIX

They came within sight of Zararis late in the afternoon.

The engines slowed down and Lord Victor realised they were to wait for the Barge which the Ambassador had told them about.

When he looked out of the port-hole he could see in the distance two lines of small sailing yachts.

They were getting into position so that the Barge could pass down between them.

There was however no sign yet of the Barge.

It was the Ambassador who suggested they should all dress early, but Lord Victor had thought it unnecessary.

This was confirmed when the Captain said in an aside:

"These people are always late. No idea of time! Never have had!"

Lord Victor knew this was true.

When he was finally dressed, he thought that in his frock-coat, stiff collar and carefully tied tie he certainly looked as was expected of a representative of the Queen.

Because there was nothing else to do, he went up on deck.

There was still no sign of the Barge which was to carry them ashore.

The sun was beginning to sink lower on the horizon and very shortly the first stars would be coming out overhead.

Last night there had been almost a full moon.

Lord Victor had deliberately not gone on deck with the Princess after dinner as he knew she wished him to do.

They had sat talking stiffly of nothing of importance until she said:

"I am going out to look at the stars!"

She walked out of the cabin as she did so.

Lord Victor was aware that the two Ladies-in-Waiting and both the men were expecting him to follow her.

Because he thought it would cause more comment if he refused, he somewhat reluctantly got to his feet.

As he expected, the Princess was in her usual place.

She was leaning against the ship's rail with the moonlight shining on her golden hair.

As Lord Victor reached her she asked in a small voice:

"Why are . . you being . . unkind to . . me?"

"I am trying to be sensible," Lord Victor replied.

"But . . I may never . . have a chance . . of being . . alone with . . you again."

"You know that tomorrow," Lord Victor answered, "we have to behave in a very different way from what has been so enjoyable these last weeks."

"I know . . I know," the Princess answered,

"but how can I . . bear it? How can I do . . all the things that are . . expected of me . . if you are . . not there?"

Lord Victor thought that the pain in her voice made it unbearable for him to go on listening to her.

He leaned over the rail some way from her and stared at the distant City.

The lights were just beginning to appear.

"I . . I am . . thinking," the Princess said, "that if I . . throw myself into the . . sea . . there would be no more . . problems."

"Now you are being over-dramatic," Lord Victor said, "and if you did such a thing, everybody would say it was my fault."

"And . . that is what . . it would be," she said beneath her breath.

Because he knew that if he stayed any longer they might both say things which they would afterwards regret, he turned away.

"I am going to my cabin," he said. "If you are wise, you will go to bed and forget about tomorrow."

He did not wait for her answer.

He felt as he walked away that he was shutting the gates of Paradise behind him.

Now this evening, as he looked out towards Zararis, he thought he had never imagined for one moment that on this voyage he would fall in love.

But it was not the joy he had expected it would be.

It was an agony, it was like a knife turning in his heart.

At last he was aware that there was something

103

moving towards them in the distance, and he knew it was Barge.

He watched it come nearer and nearer.

When finally he could see it clearly, it was different from anything he had expected.

He guessed from its appearance that it was very old.

It had perhaps been used by the Kings of Zararis ever since they had first arrived and created a Kingdom.

The Barge was painted a brilliant red and picked out in white.

It was to all intents and purposes in two tiers.

In the lower tier there were at least twenty men rowing it seated in pairs.

They looked, Lord Victor thought, like slaves locked to their seats in a Roman galley.

It would be impossible for them to stand up, since the roof which formed the upper deck was just above their heads as they sat.

This was long and wide.

The rail which was low, only about a foot high, was carved and painted in different colours.

The whole deck was massed with flowers.

Exactly in the centre on a raised platform there was a throne which was covered with flowers and fruit.

There were bunches of grapes, small oranges and peaches.

They were arranged with the brilliant coloured flowers which were characteristic of the Lower Balkan States.

There were huge pots containing small shrubs which were all in blossom.

There was also a profusion of fairy lights and lanterns which were not yet lit.

A tall mast covered with these was behind the throne on which the Princess would sit.

Lord Victor thought they had certainly done their best.

No-one could complain that they were not welcoming their future Queen in style.

He longed to discuss it with the Princess, but knew it would be a mistake to go near her.

She had looked at him reproachfully at breakfast.

He had the idea that she might have had, as he had, a more or less sleepless night.

Mr. Orestes had droned on about the history of Zararis, which he had taken upon himself to impart in every detail to the Princess.

Lord Victor did not listen.

He was quite certain that Princess Sydella was thinking only of how, if it was possible, she could talk to him alone.

This was something he was determined to avoid.

Therefore when breakfast was ended, he had gone up on the Bridge to see the Captain.

"When will you be returning to England, My Lord?" the Captain asked. "We have orders to wait for you. However, our ships are wanted here, as you will understand."

"I noticed that we passed some Battleships as we steamed up from Athens," Lord Victor remarked, "and I suspect there are more just outside the Dardanelles."

"We are just keeping an eye on things," the Captain said, "but the Russians have no wish after losing so many men on their march to Constantinople ten years ago to start another war."

"I hope you are right," Lord Victor said. "But I understand they are infiltrating wherever possible in these smaller countries."

"That is true enough," the Captain agreed. "As Your Lordship knows, there are no dirty tricks they will not get up to if they can get away with it."

Lord Victor thought this was cold comfort.

The Princess would be left in a very small country defended by what he had ascertained from the Ambassador was a ridiculously small Army.

"I have always thought we should have a Fleet of our own Battleships," the Ambassador had added, "but the Prime Minister will not incur the expense. And His Majesty believes those who tell him there is no necessity for it."

Lord Victor could only hope that Queen Victoria and the Marquess of Salisbury were right.

They were confident that the mere presence of an English Queen would keep the Russians at bay.

Princess Sydella would be extremely lonely once he had left.

Aloud he said to the Captain:

"I will let you know when I think it is expedient for me to leave. But you realise I shall have to be here for the wedding and the Coronation."

"Yes, yes, of course," the Captain agreed.

The Barge came nearer and nearer, and finally was alongside the Battleship.

Seamen appeared on the deck and managed to secure the Barge to the side of H.M.S. *Victorious*, so that it was attached without scratching the paint on either vessel.

A gang-plank was then put in place.

Lord Victor thought it was his duty to ascertain that it was safe and to be the first person to use it.

He stepped onto the deck of the Barge as its crew were busy lighting the lanterns.

They were just in time before the sun finally sank completely out of sight.

The dusk deepened quickly, as it always does in Mediterranean countries.

There was some delay while a small Orchestra arranged itself near the stern.

As they started to play a message was sent to the Princess to say that her throne of flowers was ready for her.

There were three Statesmen on the Barge.

When they greeted Lord Victor he saw they carried their speeches in their hands.

He was dismayed to see that each one consisted of half-a-dozen pages, or more.

He knew how boring it would be for the Princess.

Yet he told himself fiercely it was something to which she had to become accustomed.

When at last Princess Sydella came up on deck she was breathtakingly lovely.

It seemed wrong that the Statesmen were all in their sixties, and that he was the only young man to appreciate how exquisite she looked.

She was wearing a white gown which accentuated her tiny waist.

It was décolleté enough to reveal the whiteness of her skin.

It also showed off her long, graceful neck.

She had, Lord Victor noticed, been tactful enough not to wear jewellery.

107

Her necklace was of small white lilies, and orchids made into a wreath perched like a crown on her golden hair.

She moved slowly and with dignity over the gang-plank.

The two Baronesses followed and behind them came the Ambassador and Mr. Orestes.

The elderly Statesmen stepped forward.

As they bowed the Princess looked over their heads at Lord Victor.

He thought he saw a desperate appeal in her eyes.

He knew he could not help her.

It hurt him bitterly not to be able to do so, and as she settled herself on her flowery throne, he turned away.

The first Statesman started his speech of welcome.

Lord Victor moved to the stern of the Barge, passing the Orchestra that was now playing softly.

There was a trellis-work of flowers behind them which left him in partial darkness.

He was invisible to all the others on deck.

The moon was casting its silver rays on the sea.

Now the two lines of yachts between which the Barge was to move to the Port were ablaze with lights.

As Lord Victor stood looking at them, he suddenly became aware that something was moving below him.

He looked down to see a boat, no bigger than a canoe, beside the Barge.

There was only one man in it, and Lord Victor wondered vaguely if he was a guest arriving late.

Or else an oarsman who had missed filling his place when the Barge set sail.

Because he wanted to think of anything rather than the Princess, he watched the man ship his oars.

It was then he became aware that there was somebody in the stern of the Barge below him leaning over.

Lord Victor could not see him clearly, but the man in the boat picked up what seemed a solid article which he held up as high as he could.

Then the other man bent forward to take it from him.

Lord Victor wondered if it was something that had been left behind, perhaps a lantern.

It was then he heard the man in the boat say:

"Be very careful, and hurry!"

The man on the Barge did not reply.

But a few seconds later he sprang over the rail to join the man in the boat.

He then rowed away at what seemed to Lord Victor a quite abnormal speed.

It suddenly occurred to him that the man in the boat had spoken in Russian.

Because he could now understand it, he had not realised for the moment what language had been used.

Now as he stared after the boat, the man who had joined it from the Barge looked back.

As the moonlight shone on his face Lord Victor was almost certain it was Alexander.

It was then with a quickness of mind which was characteristic of him, he knew what they had been doing.

Running as swiftly as he could to the centre of the deck, he seized the Princess by the hand.

He pulled her from the throne.

As he did so, he shouted:

"A bomb! A bomb in the stern! Move quickly! A bomb in the stern!"

He was speaking in Greek, but as he was not certain if the word he was using was right, he repeated it in English as well.

"A bomb! A bomb!"

As he was shouting he was also running, pulling the Princess towards the bow of the Barge.

When they reached it he was almost breathless.

Through the chatter of voices behind him he said to the Princess:

"Can you swim?"

"Y.yes," she answered.

"Take off your slippers," Lord Victor ordered.

He was kicking away his own shoes as he spoke, then pulled off his tight-fitting frock-coat.

He seized the Princess once again by the hand.

As he did so he heard the first ominous sounds of an explosion behind him.

Without turning his head he drew the Princess forward and jumped.

Even as they splashed into the sea, there was a violent explosion behind them.

Then there were screams and shouts from above deck and below it.

Lord Victor did not speak.

He was swimming and at the same time supporting the Princess.

He knew she would have difficulty owing to her long gown in using her legs.

Then, as he was trying to decide in which direction

to swim, he realised that they were in the grip of a strong current.

Local currents were characteristic of the Aegean Sea.

Lord Victor had read about them.

Now involved in one, he felt it carrying them away from the Barge.

He decided it was better to go with it than try to swim against it.

Their hair was saturated by the sea, which also blinded their eyes.

As they were carried away there was another explosion.

The flash of it for the moment dazzled Lord Victor.

Now he knew he was fighting not only for his own life, but also for the Princess's.

It was many minutes later, although it seemed longer, that Lord Victor managed to manoeuvre them out of the current.

He half-supported, half-pulled the Princess with him.

He was fortunately a very strong swimmer, and it was something he had enjoyed whenever he had the opportunity.

Finally they were in smoother water and Lord Victor spoke for the first time.

"Take it slowly," he said. "We must not exhaust ourselves."

The Princess did not answer, but her fingers tightened on his.

He wondered how long she would manage to stay afloat without any further assistance.

Then unexpectedly he was aware that they were

in sheltered water and as he put down his foot he found there was sand beneath it.

Now he could see the outline of a small cove.

He pulled the Princess towards it.

A few seconds later they were treading in only a foot or so of water.

They were soon on a sandy beach enclosed by a bay.

Lord Victor straightened himself and turned towards the Princess.

She took one step forward, then her arms were round his neck.

"You . . have . . saved . . me! You have . . saved . . me!" she cried.

Her face was lifted up to his.

For the moment it was impossible to think clearly.

Lord Victor was only aware that they were both alive and he drew her close to him.

Then his lips were on hers.

Their faces were wet from the sea water, and for a moment their lips were cold.

Then as Lord Victor felt the Princess moving closer to him his kiss became demanding, possessive and finally passionate.

He kissed her as he had longed to do, until he felt that he made her his.

To Princess Sydella it was as if he took her heart from her body, and she gave him her soul also.

Only when at last Lord Victor raised his head did she say in a voice that seemed like the song of the angels:

"I . . love . . y.you . . I l.love . . you!"

It was then that Lord Victor came back to reality.

"My darling," he said hoarsely, "those devils might have killed you."

"But . . you saved . . me . . you s.saved me," she whispered.

"We were saved only because I have learnt Russian," he said.

"Was it . . the Russians?" the Princess queried. "They . . wanted to . . kill . . me?"

"It was Alexander who planted the bomb in the Barge," Lord Victor said in a harsh voice.

"Alexander!" the Princess exclaimed. "I told you he had hard eyes . . but I did not think he would try to . . kill me!"

"What they wanted," Lord Victor said, "was to prevent there being an English Queen on the throne of Zararis."

He gave a deep sigh.

"But they failed!"

He looked back and could just see the Battleship much further away than he expected.

It was silhouetted against the fire on the Barge blazing on the far side of it.

He was certain there were sights there that the Princess should not see.

It was also obvious they could not get back to it anyway.

He turned round saying:

"Now we had better explore and see if there is somewhere where we can at least dry ourselves."

He was thinking that inland there might be crofts of some sort.

But there were no lights, in fact no sign of human beings.

They walked along the shore and suddenly Lord Victor gave an exclamation.

Just at the end of the bay, somewhat above the beach, was a small hut.

Lord Victor thought it was probably a boat-shed of some sort.

But at least it was somewhere where they could dry themselves and wait to be rescued.

The Princess saw the hut almost at the same time that he did.

"A little hut!" she exclaimed. "Do you think there might be somebody in it?"

"If there is, I think by this time they would have come out to see what was happening out at sea," Lord Victor replied.

They reached the hut and he saw there was a double door behind which he suspected there lay a boat.

There was also, and this was helpful, a comparatively large glass-paned window.

Lord Victor first ascertained that the door was locked.

The Princess sat down on a rock to watch him as he broke a pane of glass in the window.

"Be careful not to cut yourself!" she warned.

"I really should have something to cover my hand," Lord Victor replied.

The Princess gave a little cry.

"I will give you something . . but do not . . look round."

He guessed what she was about to do and waited obediently.

A few moments later she handed him a silk petticoat edged with lace.

"I will try not to tear it," he promised.

He could see in the moonlight that she was smiling, and he added:

"Even in such an emergency, I am sure the 'Watch-dogs' would consider it very improper for me to accept it!"

The Princess gave a chuckle, and he thought no woman could be more brave and cool-headed.

He could not imagine that any of the Beauties he had known in the past would not have screamed and protested when he wanted them to jump into the sea.

He was quite certain that now they would be crying on his shoulder.

Making him realise they wished to be comforted.

He cleared away the broken glass still in the frame and managed to open the window.

The Princess's silk petticoat wrapped round his hand protected it.

Once he had the window open, he swung himself inside.

It was then he found that the hut was larger than he had at first expected.

It took him only a short time to find what he sought.

On a shelf he found a candle, and beside it an oil-lamp.

Looking about Lord Victor saw that the hut was used by its owner not only to house his boat.

He must sometimes have stayed there.

In fact Lord Victor guessed the hut belonged to a man who enjoyed yachting as a hobby whenever he had the opportunity.

Once he had lit the candle and lantern Lord

Victor lifted the Princess through the window-frame.

As he did so he realised how wet she was.

Although it was a warm night she was shivering a little.

"Undress quickly!" he commanded. "I am sure I can find you something to wear."

There was a cupboard at one end of the hut which was locked.

Lord Victor with great ingenuity managed to break it open.

As he had hoped, there were towels, blankets and a towelling dressing-gown which the owner had obviously used after bathing.

Lord Victor took it to the Princess.

He saw as he reached her that she had obeyed his order and taken off the pretty white lace-trimmed gown she had worn on the Barge.

She had in fact, as she had given him her petticoat, very little left to wear.

Quickly he handed her the dressing-gown and turned away.

"You are to take off your wet clothes too," the Princess said, "or else you will catch cold, and that will be very unbecoming!"

Lord Victor laughed.

He thought again that no other woman could have been so light-hearted and sensible as the Princess was being.

He went back to the cupboard and found a shirt and a pair of trousers.

He guessed the owner had worn them when sailing his boat, rather than spoil the clothes in which he had arrived.

Lord Victor changed quickly.

Then he discovered there was an ancient contraption on which it would be possible to cook.

It would also dry their clothes if they were laid around it.

He told the Princess of his discovery.

She came to his side and asked:

"Do you know how to work that funny-looking stove?"

"I expect I can find out," Lord Victor replied, "although of course the cooking is your job!"

The Princess laughed.

"Is there anything to cook? I should have thought it was rather too late to go fishing."

As if she had challenged him, Lord Victor searched at the back of the cupboard.

He discovered a saucepan, a kettle and a tin that contained coffee.

There were mugs to drink from.

"I will make the coffee," the Princess said. "You take out the blankets."

Lord Victor looked around to see where they could sleep.

In one corner there was a wooden bedstead with a straw mattress on it.

As he unfolded the blankets he thought how fortunate they were not to be still shivering in the night air in their wet clothes with no shelter.

As he looked for a cushion or a pillow the Princess said:

"I suppose you realise that although we have some coffee, there is no water to boil in the kettle!"

"I never thought of that!" Lord Victor admitted. "I expect the owner of the hut brings his own fresh water with him."

"There might be a spring outside the back door," the Princess suggested.

Lord Victor smiled.

"I will go and look."

He had actually not expected there to be another entrance to the hut.

But he found a small door and thought he had been very remiss.

It was bolted so that it could not have been opened from the outside.

When he went out he found that the Princess had been cleverer than he expected.

There was a rough pump which had obviously been made by an amateur builder, but it worked.

It took him some time to pump up enough water to fill the kettle.

It took a lot of effort to make the water clean, which must have come from an inland stream.

However if they boiled the water, it should be safe to drink.

The Princess was delighted.

She carried it away to the stove.

When she managed to make two mugs of coffee she was very pleased with herself.

"This is what I would be doing if I was marrying a poor man," she said.

She was speaking spontaneously as she always did.

As the words passed her lips it struck them both that this was something she would never have to do again.

She was not marrying a poor man, she was marrying a King.

He was waiting for her at this very moment in his Palace.

Because the Princess knew what Lord Victor was thinking, she said quickly:

"How stupid of . . me! It was . . something I might have . . said at . . home, but not . . here."

She put down her mug and said in a soft voice:

"They will not . . find us until . . tomorrow, and now . . I am . . here with . . you."

She moved towards him and he knew what she wanted.

"No!" he said sharply. "You must forget what happened just now!"

"Why should I forget the most . . wonderful thing that has ever . . happened . . to me?" the Princess asked.

Lord Victor did not answer and she went on:

"I always thought . . a kiss would be . . wonderful, but not so . . marvellous . . so utterly and completely . . perfect that I shall . . never forget it."

"I want you to remember it," Lord Victor said, "but it is something that must not happen again."

"But . . why . . why?" the Princess asked. "I love you . . and we are . . here alone . . in a world of . . our own . . and it could be a . . long time before anyone . . finds us."

"As soon as they do," Lord Victor said, "you will become a Queen."

"That could happen . . tomorrow . . the day after . . or the day after that!" the Princess said wildly. "What I am thinking . . about is now . . this moment . . when the world . . is far away . . blown up by a bomb . . from which you . . saved me."

She put out her hands towards him.

Lord Victor knew that she was so innocent that

119

she had no idea how cruelly, in effect, she was tempting him.

Only by a superhuman effort did he stop himself from sweeping her into his arms.

Instead he kissed her hands, first one, then the other.

As if he could not help himself, he turned the hand he was holding and kissed her palm.

He knew that she quivered and the thrill that ran through her was very obvious.

It was then he said in a deep voice:

"I love you, my darling, I love you as I have never loved anyone before and will never love anyone again, but I am also a gentleman, and as a gentleman, I cannot touch you."

As he finished speaking, he walked towards the back door.

"Go to bed," he said, "and go to sleep. I am leaving you alone because I love you too much to hurt you."

He was gone.

The Princess knew she must not follow him.

CHAPTER SEVEN

Lord Victor walked down onto the sand and sat on a rock looking out to sea.

The flames from the Barge were still rising in the far distance.

He however was looking with unseeing eyes in front of him.

The moon and the stars were reflected in the water, but he was aware only of the darkness which was beginning to encompass him.

Gradually the rapture that the Princess had aroused faded away.

There remained only despair and fear for the future.

He must have been there for quite a long time when suddenly he heard a scream.

He jumped to his feet and as he did so he heard the Princess scream again.

He ran across the sand.

As he got near to the Boat-House he saw a man peering in through the broken window.

He turned round as Lord Victor approached and the moonlight was on his face.

Lord Victor saw that he was an old, strange-looking creature.

As he rushed away into the darkness, his clothes flapping round him, it was obvious he was no more than a scavenger.

Lord Victor pulled open the back door and as he did so the Princess threw herself against him.

"It is . . the Russians! The . . Russians!" she cried. "They are . . trying to . . kill me!"

Lord Victor held her close.

"It is all right, my darling," he said, "it is not the Russians, only a scavenger."

"I . . I am . . frightened!" the Princess faltered and burst into tears.

She cried tempestuously like a child.

Lord Victor picked her up in his arms and carried her to the bed.

He would have set her down, but she clung to him saying:

"Do not . . leave me! Please . . do not leave . . me!"

"I am not going to leave you, my Precious. I should not have gone away in the first place."

He laid her down and pulled half of a blanket over her.

Then lying on top of the other half he put his arm around her so that her head was on his shoulder.

He pulled another blanket over himself.

The Princess was still crying and he held her very close to him saying:

"It is all right, my sweet, my darling, it was only a scavenger looking for something to steal."

"B.But . . the R.Russians . . tried to . . k.kill me when I was . . on the . . Barge," the Princess stammered.

"I know that," Lord Victor agreed, "but we

will make certain it will not happen again."

"But . . how . . how?"

The words seemed almost incoherent and he could feel her whole body trembling against him.

Because there was no answer to her question he turned her face up to his and kissed her.

It was a very gentle kiss, but he knew it brought back the ecstasy she had felt before.

Gradually, she was no longer trembling, but quivering to his kisses.

"I . . I love . . you!" she said a little later, and now the fear was gone from her voice.

"And I love you!" Lord Victor replied.

The Princess raised her hand to touch his cheek.

"Let us run away," she whispered. "If we ran away . . where . . no-one could . . find us . . we could be . . together . . and perhaps . . they will think we were . . drowned in . . the sea."

Lord Victor kissed her forehead.

"Do you think we, of all people, could actually do that, my Precious?" he asked. "Whatever we may feel about ourselves, our country has to come first. It is the same as if we were soldiers and we refused to fight the enemy. Then we would be traitors, and that is something I could never allow you to be."

"But . . I cannot . . lose you," the Princess murmured. "Promise that . . you will . . stay for as long as . . you can to . . protect me."

The fear was back in her voice and Lord Victor said quietly:

"I will stay for as long as it is possible for me to do so."

. . . .

The light of the first fingers of the dawn coming through the broken window made Lord Victor aware that soon the sailors from the H.M.S. *Victorious* would be searching for them.

The Princess had fallen asleep.

He, however, had lain awake wondering desperately what he could do to ensure her safety and her happiness.

Now he removed his arm gently so as not to disturb her and walked towards the window.

The candle had guttered out in the early hours of the morning.

The lantern, running out of oil, had followed.

He was aware however that the stove was still burning.

Their clothes draped around it had dried by now.

He glanced back at the bed.

As the Princess was still sleeping, he changed back into his own clothes.

They were somewhat the worse for wear after their soaking in the sea.

But at least he was more presentable than he had been in the clothes he had borrowed and which did not fit him.

As he finished dressing he saw a boat coming down the coast.

He went to the Princess and bending down kissed her very gently.

"Wake up, my darling," he said. "We are about to be rescued, and you must dress."

She lifted her arms towards him, but he moved towards the door.

"We have to go back to civilisation," he said, "so hurry!"

He walked across the sands as he had done the night before.

As he reached the waves coming in he saw that the boat was only a short distance from him.

He waved his arms and the seamen, who were under the direction of a Junior Officer, waved back.

It took them only a few minutes to reach the shore and the Officer sprang from the boat.

"Are you all right, M'Lord?" he asked. "Her Royal Highness is with you?"

"We were fortunate enough to find shelter in a hut," Lord Victor explained, "and we passed the night there, but of course, it has been a tremendous shock to Her Royal Highness."

He said the same thing half-an-hour later when they had reached H.M.S. *Victorious*.

The Princess had gone directly to her cabin.

The Captain had come to his cabin.

Lord Victor had wrapped himself in a comfortable robe and was eating breakfast which had been brought to him on a tray.

"You not only saved your own life and that of Her Royal Highness, My Lord," the Captain said, "but a number of other people are exceedingly grateful that your warning gave them time to get aboard my ship."

"What are the casualties, Captain?" Lord Victor enquired.

He had not asked this question immediately on coming aboard.

He had been too intent on getting the Princess to her cabin without her having a conversation with anybody.

He was afraid that she might break down again and cling to him.

Yet although she was very pale, she carried herself proudly.

"I am afraid, My Lord," the Captain replied, "that the two Ladies-in-Waiting were both killed, also two of the Statesmen who had come to welcome her on the Barge. The third is badly injured and has been taken to Hospital."

Lord Victor was aware this was because they were old and obviously could not run to safety.

"The Ambassador," the Captain went on, "has a bad bruise on his forehead, and Mr. Orestes has an injured arm."

He paused before he added:

"Twenty-two people in all were killed by the bomb, or else drowned in the sea. There might have been many more if it had not been for Your Lordship's timely warning."

"Did you realise that it was Alexander who planted the bomb on the Barge?" Lord Victor asked.

"I did not know that," the Captain answered, "but I wondered what had happened to him when it was reported to me that he had disappeared. I have always said you cannot trust the Russians!"

"They were trying to kill the Princess before she could become Queen of Zararis," Lord Victor replied.

"That is what I thought myself," the Captain said, "and I have already arranged that I will now take my ship straight into the harbour. We must also make certain that Her Royal Highness is properly protected until she is crowned."

Lord Victor nodded.

He knew, without saying so, that once the Princess was on the throne the Russians would not risk a war with England by destroying her.

They might therefore make another attempt to kill her before she became Queen.

He thought it unlikely, and yet it was something which could not be ignored.

"Now, this is what I suggest you do .." he said to the Captain.

. . . .

The crowds were cheering wildly.

Princess Sydella, in an open carriage, was driving down the main street which led from the Quay to the Palace.

A number of children had small Union Jacks to wave.

The trees on either side of the road were decorated not only with flowers, but also with flags and bunting.

Opposite Her Royal Highness with their backs to the horses sat Lord Victor and the Captain, both armed unobtrusively with revolvers.

On the road on each side of the carriage marched a picked detachment of the ship's company.

They were all of them, as Lord Victor was aware, excited at being part of what they knew was a blow against an invisible enemy.

There were soldiers lining the route, but, Lord Victor thought scornfully, not nearly enough.

There were more, he was glad to see, outside the Palace, which was a very attractive building.

It was white and set against a background of trees in blossom.

Two huge fountains were playing, one on each side of the marble steps which led up to the front door.

"Have we to climb all those steps?" the Princess asked.

She was waving her hand and bowing to the cheering populace on each side of the road.

"I am afraid so," Lord Victor answered, "and the King, the Prime Minister, and a lot of other dignitaries will be waiting for you at the top of them."

"You .. you will .. walk up .. with me?" the Princess asked nervously.

"Of course," Lord Victor replied, "and the Captain and I will make sure you are not harmed in any way."

He knew as he spoke that she was frightened, but he thought that nobody could have behaved better than she was doing at this moment.

She looked outstandingly beautiful.

She had a little hat perched at the back of her head trimmed with feathers.

She was all in white and only her bouquet was of pink roses to make a splash of colour.

As her eyes met Lord Victor's he knew she was pleading with him to help her.

He bent forward to say quietly:

"Everything is arranged, and I will be beside you in case there is anything you want."

He knew that was what she wanted to hear, and he saw the light come into her eyes.

They had not been alone together since he had taken her back to the Ship.

But he could read her thoughts, and he knew she was wishing that at the last minute they could run away together into obscurity.

The carriage came to a standstill.

A footman in elaborate livery ran to open the

carriage-door.

As the Princess stepped out the crew from the Battleship presented arms, then raised their caps as they gave three cheers.

Lord Victor and the Captain followed closely behind her.

When they reached the top of the steps there was a man standing outside the glass door that led into the Palace.

Lord Victor expected it to be the King, but it was the Prime Minister.

When the Princess reached him he bowed low and kissed her hand.

Then he said in a very serious tone:

"I must ask you, Your Royal Highness, to come into a Reception-Room where there are several people waiting to meet you."

The Princess did not seem surprised.

Lord Victor however thought it extraordinary that there was as yet no sign of the King.

The Prime Minister led the way with the Princess, Lord Victor and the Captain walking behind him.

They were aware as they did so that the Palace was very attractively built.

The furniture and pictures they noticed as they passed were exceptionally fine.

The Prime Minister opened the door of what was a comparatively small room.

Waiting for them was the Ambassador and Mr. Orestes with a Priest whom Lord Victor thought was the Archbishop.

There was also the Lord Chamberlain, the Comptroller of the Household, a bemedalled General, an Admiral and three other men who Lord Victor guessed were Members of the Privy Council.

Then the door was shut behind them and the Prime Minister said:

"May I, Your Royal Highness, present the Archbishop of Zararis."

The Princess shook the Archbishop by the hand.

One after another the other men were then presented to her.

She of course already knew the Ambassador and Mr. Orestes.

The Prime Minister indicated a chair on which the Princess could sit before they surrounded her in a half-circle.

Lord Victor could not imagine what all this was about.

Then the Prime Minister said:

"I have the sad task, Your Royal Highness, of bringing you exceedingly distressing news."

The Princess looked up in surprise as he went on:

"I regret to inform Your Royal Highness that His Majesty, who has not been well for some time, died last night."

Lord Victor started.

Then, as he knew that the Princess was at a loss for words, he went to her side.

She was finding it difficult to speak and he said:

"This is indeed grave news, Mr. Prime Minister, and a tremendous shock to Her Royal Highness on top of everything that has already occurred."

"I am aware of that, My Lord," the Prime Minister replied, "but I think you will understand that because of the most regrettable occurrence on Her Royal Highness's arrival, we have had to keep secret the news of His Majesty's death until this moment."

"And is no-one else aware that he is dead?" Lord Victor asked.

"His personal servants and the doctors have been sworn to secrecy, and we here present are the only other people who know the truth . ."

Lord Victor did not say anything more. After a moment the Prime Minister said to the Princess:

"Your Royal Highness must be aware that if this situation is known, the Russians will do everything possible to prevent us from appointing another Royal Ruler of Zararis. We are therefore begging Your Royal Highness to take the throne and do us the very great honour of becoming our Queen."

The Princess gave a gasp of horror and Lord Victor said quickly:

"Are you saying, Prime Minister, that if Her Royal Highness becomes Queen the Russians will accept that Zararis is under the protection of the British Empire and their efforts to infiltrate and disturb the country will cease?"

"You are putting into words what I actually would have said myself, My Lord," the Prime Minister replied, "and I profoundly hope that you, as the representative of Her Majesty Queen Victoria will persuade the Princess to take the throne of Zararis, and save us from our enemies."

As he spoke Princess Sydella reached out and slipped her hand into Lord Victor's.

"I . . I am deeply . . grieved to learn of . . His Majesty's . . death," she said in a small hesitating voice, "and while I am . . aware of the great . . honour you do me in . . offering me . . the throne,

I could not . . contemplate being just by myself in such a . . responsible position . . in fact . . I would . . not know . . what to . . do."

Lord Victor saw the consternation in the Prime Minister's face and in those of the other men present.

He knew they were aware, as the Marquess of Salisbury had told him, how vulnerable Zararis was.

If there was no-one at all on the throne, let alone someone British, the Russians would all the more stir up trouble, as they already had done elsewhere.

He was wondering if he should suggest that he spoke to the Princess alone.

However, before he could say anything, she rose to her feet.

"Thank you," she said, "for what . . you have . . offered, but I would . . like to . . go home."

The Prime Minister stepped forward as if he would physically prevent her from leaving.

Then he said, the words falling over themselves:

"I am sure, Your Royal Highness, we can find some member of His Late Majesty's family who would be willing to be crowned King, if you would stay here as his bride."

He turned to the Archbishop saying:

"What about Prince Frederick? You have seen him in the last year?"

"He is not in good health," the Archbishop replied, "and is, as you know, a recluse, but of course you could approach him."

The Princess turned to Lord Victor.

"No, no," she protested. "I cannot . . marry . . any . . one. Please . . take me . . home!"

It was the cry of a child.

Then as Lord Victor hesitated, not knowing what

to say, she gave a sudden exclamation.

Still holding onto his hand, she turned towards the Prime Minister.

"If . . you want . . a King," she said, "why not . . Lord Victor Brooke? He is . . a descendant of an . . English King and . . like me, has Queen Victoria as his . . Godmother."

The Prime Minister stared at her and Mr. Orestes, who had his arm in a sling, moved forward.

"This is extraordinary," he said, "because I have been working on the Lineage of His Lordship.

"Charles II became King of England at the Restoration in 1660. Later he made his son, by his mistress Nell Gwyn, the Duke of St. Albans. Lord Victor Brooke's Mother, the Duchess of Droxbrooke, was the sister of the late Duke of St. Albans, his direct descendant, and is Aunt of the present Duke."

There was an exclamation from the other Statesmen while the Prime Minister's expression changed.

He looked towards Lord Victor and said:

"In which case, My Lord, I speak with confidence on behalf of the people of Zararis, and of the House of Parliament, I beg of you to accept the throne of Zararis, and to preserve and protect this country under the patronage of The British Empire and Her Majesty Queen Victoria."

Then there was a pause and the Princess turned to look at Lord Victor anxiously.

Then there was complete silence while everyone seemed to be holding their breath.

"Please, please," the Princess whispered.

After what seemed a long pause Lord Victor said slowly, "Thank you for the trust with which you honour me. With the help of God, I will endeavour to serve this country and its people."

The Prime Minister went down on one knee.

"The King is dead!" he said. "Long live the King!"

Taking Lord Victor's hand he raised it to his lips.

Each of the other men present followed his example.

As the last one rose to his feet, Lord Victor said:

"If I am to become your King, I will now announce what I require to be done to make sure that my future wife is safe and that you need no longer as a country walk in fear."

He drew in his breath before looking at the Archbishop and saying:

"I want, My Lord, our marriage to take place tomorrow at two o'clock, and that we should be crowned immediately afterwards."

He then turned towards the General saying:

"Every available soldier in the country is to line the route, and I want you, General, to immediately enlist every able-bodied young man into the Armed Forces, some will be required for the Navy."

The General bowed an acceptance of the order, and Lord Victor went on:

"The Prime Minister will announce Conscription for every boy of seventeen for at least three years."

Lord Victor paused before he continued:

"I direct, Admiral, that two Battleships and three Destroyers should be placed on order from England. Arrangements must be made for the crews who will man them to begin training immediately."

There was a gasp from those who were listening.

Then Lord Victor said, in a different tone:

"As my future wife has been through a very traumatic experience, and neither of us had any sleep last night, we will now retire to our private apartments, and any celebrations as regards our wedding can take place tomorrow."

He looked round at the men who were all staring at him and said:

"I feel sure I can leave the sacred burial of His Majesty in your hands, and that you, Prime Minister, will announce to the people tomorrow at mid-day, and not before, that, following His Majesty's death there is a National Emergency, and it is for this reason that our marriage will take place immediately."

As he stopped speaking, Lord Victor offered his arm to the Princess, and they walked towards the door.

Realising they were leaving, the Comptroller of the Household hurried to open it for them.

Outside there were a number of footmen, servants and Palace officials.

As they bowed, the Comptroller said:

"I will show Her Royal Highness to her private apartments."

He walked ahead.

Lord Victor was aware that the Princess was worried that she might be parted from him.

He put his right hand over hers which was on his arm.

She knew he was telling her without words that he would never leave her.

Then as he saw the radiance in her eyes he knew that for the Princess as well as for himself, the stars were glittering.

They were all around them.

However, they were no longer on earth, but flying up to the sky.

CHAPTER EIGHT

The Comptroller of the Household opened a door and showed the Princess and Lord Victor into a most impressive bed-room.

Two maids were already unpacking the Princess's luggage which had been brought ashore from the ship.

"These are Your Royal Highness's apartments," the Comptroller said, "the Sitting-Room, ma'am, is next door."

He walked across to the communicating door and Lord Victor said very quietly to the Princess:

"Stay here for a moment."

He saw the apprehension in her eyes and added:

"I am not leaving you, I just want to talk to him alone."

She nodded to say she understood.

Lord Victor joined the Comptroller in an attractive and comfortable Sitting-Room.

As Lord Victor came to his side, the Comptroller said:

"You understand, My Lord, that this is not the Royal Suite, because obviously it cannot be used at the moment."

"No, no, of course, I understand," Lord Victor replied.

Then lowering his voice he went on:

"Tonight I wish to be near the Princess, and I imagine there is another room attached to this one?"

The Comptroller looked at him apprehensively.

"Do you really think . . . ?" he began.

"I am taking no risks," Lord Victor interrupted, "and I have already arranged with the Captain of H.M.S. *Victorious* for a detachment of men to be here on guard."

As he was afraid the Comptroller would think it an insult to his soldiers he added:

"I want this whole floor guarded so that no-one – no-one at all – including yourself, can approach us once Her Royal Highness has gone to bed."

"I will see to that," the Comptroller agreed.

"What we require now," Lord Victor went on, "is in an hour or so to have a light meal served in this room, and after that I want the Princess to have as much sleep as possible."

"Your wishes will be carried out, My Lord," the Comptroller said.

He showed Lord Victor a bed-room which was on the other side of the Sitting-Room.

It was almost as impressive as the one the Princess was using.

Lord Victor asked that his Valet and his luggage be sent there, then went back into the Sitting-Room.

When the Comptroller left, bowing respectfully, he called to the Princess.

She came running from the bed-room.

"Is . . everything all . . right?" she asked.

"Everything, my Darling," Lord Victor said, "but I am just wondering how you managed to get me into a position I never expected – even in my wildest dreams!"

"I . . I just wanted to . . be with you," the Princess said, "it does not matter to me whether . . you are a King, or a crossing-sweeper, as . . long as . . we are . . together."

Lord Victor thought that no man could ask more of any woman.

He took the Princess's hand and raised it to his lips.

The Princess moved away from him and shut the door that led into the bed-room.

Then as he waited she came back to him looking, he thought, dazzlingly lovely.

She stood beside him before she asked:

"You are . . quite sure . . that you . . really want to . . marry me?"

Lord Victor smiled.

He knew the question was very important to her.

"I want it more than I have ever wanted anything in my whole life," he said. "But I thought last night I would have to go home alone, missing you unbearably. I knew too I now could never marry."

The Princess gave a little cry of relief.

"That is . . what I wanted . . you to say . . ! Oh, Darling, Darling Victor, how can . . we have been . . so lucky?"

She put her arms around his neck and pulled his head down to hers.

Then he was kissing her fiercely, possessively, passionately until they were both breathless.

An hour later they had a light but delicious meal

– Lord Victor thought it almost as good as any food he had eaten in France.

When they had finished he said:

"Now my Lovely One, I want you to go to bed, and when you are undressed I have something to explain to you."

The Princess looked curious, but Lord Victor walked away towards his own room.

He had already given his orders.

He knew that his Valet and the maids who were looking after the Princess would already have left the floor.

He nevertheless looked out into the corridor to make sure there was no-one about.

He could see in the distance that the sailors from H.M.S. *Victorious* were standing guard.

He knew that it would be impossible for anyone to pass them.

He undressed and changed into a long robe, then returned to the Princess.

She was wearing a pretty négligée of blue satin, trimmed with Valencian lace.

Her hair was loose and fell over her shoulders.

As she ran towards him he thought no-one could look more beautiful.

However he only kissed her gently, then taking his arms from her said:

"Now, my Precious, I want you to do exactly what I tell you."

"You . . know I . . will do . . that," the Princess answered, "as I always . . will."

It was with difficulty that Lord Victor refrained from kissing her again.

Instead he went to her bed.

Picking up one of the pillows and a silk-covered Eiderdown, he carried them into the Sitting-Room.

"What are . . you doing?" the Princess asked.

"I think you will be very comfortable on this sofa," he said, "and as it is so warm tonight, you will not need any blankets."

The Princess was staring at him in astonishment.

"You mean . . I am to . . sleep . . here?"

"Yes, my Darling," Lord Victor said.

The Princess's eyes were dark as she asked:

"You . . you think that . . perhaps . . oh, Victor, you do not . . think . . the Russians will . . try to . . k.kill me . . again?"

Lord Victor put his arms around her.

"I think that having failed dismally once they will not risk being made to look foolish a second time," he said, "but because I love you and because you are everything in the world to me, I am going to guard you, as the most precious and valuable person in the whole world."

He spoke in a deep voice which was very moving.

The Princess pressed her cheek against his shoulder.

"Once we are married," Lord Victor said, "and we are King and Queen of this country, we need no longer be afraid, but I intend to watch over you every minute of tonight until dawn."

He pulled her a little closer to him and added:

"And tomorrow night you will sleep in my arms."

"I did . . that last . . night," the Princess whispered.

"But not close enough!" Lord Victor answered, "and tomorrow it will be very, very different."

He knew that in her innocence she did not understand what he was saying.

Nor did she know what a superhuman effort it had been last night for him not to make her his.

But he worshipped her purity and he merely kissed her forehead and said:

"Lie down on the sofa, my Precious, because if you are tired, so am I."

"Of course . . you are," the Princess agreed, "but . . where do . . you intend . . to sleep?"

"In your room," Lord Victor replied, "but the door will be left open so that if you call me in the night, I will come at once."

"That is . . what I wanted . . to know," the Princess said.

She settled herself on the sofa and laid her head on the pillow.

Lord Victor arranged the Eiderdown over her.

Then he knelt down beside her and kissed her gently.

"After you have said your prayers," he said, "dream of me, and tomorrow our dreams will all come true."

He kissed her forehead, her eyes, her little nose and lastly her lips.

Her breath was coming quickly and Lord Victor felt the blood throbbing in his temples.

He forced himself to rise and went to his bedroom.

He took the bolster from the bed and two pillows.

He blew out the lights after first seeing that the door into the passage was locked.

As he passed through the Sitting-Room he could see that the Princess was already asleep.

He therefore walked softly so as not to disturb her.

He blew out the candles and went into her bed-room.

There he put the bolster down the centre of the bed, leaving the end of it resting on a pillow.

He contemplated it for a moment, then went to the wash-hand-stand.

From there he collected a large sponge which he placed at the end of the bolster.

It would look like the hair on a woman's head as long as the room was in semi-darkness.

Then he drew up the bed-clothes and blew out the lights by the bed.

There was a large sofa at the far end of the room which was much the same as the one on which the Princess was sleeping.

Lord Victor pushed it as far as it would go into a corner.

He then arranged one pillow for his head and put the other down on the floor.

As it was a warm night the windows were open although the curtains had been drawn.

Lord Victor blew out the remaining lights which were on the dressing-table.

Then he drew back one of the curtains slightly.

Now there was just enough light for anyone to be aware there was a person asleep in the four-poster bed.

Lord Victor went to the sofa in the corner of the room.

After taking his revolver from the pocket of his

robe and putting it within reach of his hand he lay down.

The room was in darkness save for one shaft of moonlight coming through the curtains.

Lord Victor felt extremely sleepy.

He had been awake all last night and had not relaxed for a second during the day.

He felt his eyes begin to close.

At the same time he knew that if there was any sound to be heard he was a very light sleeper.

It must have been two hours later when Lord Victor was dreaming of the Princess that he was suddenly awake.

As he opened his eyes he became completely alert.

He told himself there could be no reason to worry.

Yet instinctively he knew that something was wrong.

He kept very still.

It was then he heard a very faint sound.

He thought it had come from the adjoining room where Princess Sydella was sleeping.

He was just about to spring up and investigate when the sound came again.

Now he was aware that it came from outside his window.

It was then he realised that somebody was climbing up the outer wall of the Palace.

It was a feat which he would have thought impossible.

Yet he knew now that someone intended to enter the room by the window.

Keeping very still, hardly daring to breathe, Lord Victor waited.

Now there was no question but that there was somebody just outside.

So silently that it was uncanny, the moonlight was blotted out and a man came through the open window into the bedroom.

Lord Victor still did not move.

He could see what was little more than the shadow of a man moving stealthily and without making a sound towards the bed.

There was just a flash of silver as the intruder raised the knife he had in his hand.

Levelling his revolver Lord Victor held the pillow immediately in front of it and fired.

With the sure aim of an outstanding game-shot, his bullet hit the man by the bed in the back of his head.

Lord Victor fired again, to make quite certain that he was dead.

He then sprang up from the sofa.

He went first to the door leading into the Princess's room and closed it.

It was a relief to see that because he had fired through the pillow she had not been disturbed.

He then pulled back the curtains so that the moonlight flowed into the room.

He could see that the man he had shot had collapsed on the floor beside the bed.

Lord Victor looked down and saw he was wearing the uniform of a British sailor.

For the passing of a second he was desperately afraid he had made a mistake.

Then as he turned the man over he recognised Alexander.

144

Lord Victor had no intention of allowing Princess Sydella to drive to the Cathedral alone as was correct.

He gave orders that they would drive together.

Their carriage was to be accompanied by Cavalry from the moment it left the Palace.

He also sent for the General in charge of the troops guarding the streets.

He went over with him every place on the way to the Cathedral which might prove to be dangerous.

"We have never had so many troops on guard before," the General said, as if he thought Lord Victor was being needlessly apprehensive.

However Lord Victor had no intention of telling him what had happened last night, but he said firmly:

"I have reason to think Her Royal Highness and myself will be in danger until we are actually married and crowned. I therefore intend to take every possible precaution."

He thought for a moment and then asked:

"I presume the coachmen driving the carriage have all been checked and also those in attendance on us before and during the ceremony?"

He was well aware that the General thought he was being fussy.

However he gave direct orders which could not be disobeyed.

There was always a chance that the Russians might make one more great effort.

If this could rid them of the King and Queen it would leave the country defenceless.

It would also give them time to move in before anything could be done by the outside world.

Lord Victor dressed in what appeared to him to be an over-medalled and over-decorated uniform.

He then went to Princess Sydella's bed-room to see if she was alright.

She was unaware of anything that had happened during the night and she smiled at him as he entered.

'She was,' he thought, 'looking exceedingly lovely.'

Her white gown which she had brought with her from England was embroidered with diamanté around the décolletage and the hem.

Over it was a priceless Brussels lace veil which swept to the ground.

It was kept in place by a huge tiara which she would wear until it was replaced by the Crown.

When he entered the room the Ladies-in-Waiting withdrew tactfully and so did the ladies-maids.

As the door shut behind them the Princess held out both hands.

"Nothing happened during the night," she said, "and I slept peacefully."

"That is what I wanted you to do my Darling," Lord Victor replied.

She rose from the stool in front of the dressing table and said:

"Do I look alright, am I pretty enough for you?"

"It is difficult for me to tell you how lovely you are," Lord Victor said. "But my Precious, God has been very kind and tonight you will be my wife and

146

for the first time I can tell you how much I love you without feeling guilty."

The Princess laughed and then she lifted her lips to his.

Very slowly as if he was savouring the moment he drew her close to him.

Then as he kissed her the rapture they had felt before carried them wildly into the sky.

With the greatest difficulty Lord Victor released the Princess saying in a voice that was deep and a little unsteady:

"We shall have to leave in a short time."

"Am I going with you in the same carriage?" the Princess managed to ask.

Her face was radiant, her eyes shining.

Lord Victor thought it was impossible for any woman to look so lovely.

"We shall be together," he said quietly, "as we always shall be from now on. And we have my Precious a great deal for which to be thankful."

"I thanked God last night and I thanked Him again this morning," Princess Sydella said. "Oh! Victor I never thought, I never dreamt I would be able to marry you. Are you quite certain you want me?"

"Do not ask such a ridiculous question," Lord Victor answered. "I will tell you exactly how much I love you as soon as you are my wife."

He kissed her again very gently.

He knew the fire that was burning in both of them was very near the surface.

As he left the room the servants came crowding back to finish getting the Princess ready.

There was a train which hung from her shoulders

which was made of ermine and embroidered with diamanté to match her gown.

There was a diamond necklace which was part of the Crown Jewels to wear round her neck.

A bracelet for each of her small wrists.

She took a last look in the mirror.

She prayed that Lord Victor would think her more beautiful than the women with whom he had spent his time in Paris and those whom he was interested in in London.

'I love him, I love him' she told herself. 'Although it may be difficult for him to give up his own country and be here with me, I must just pray I can make him happy and never regret staying as King.'

There was a tap on the door and a maid told her Lord Victor was waiting below.

She hurried down the stairs.

Two Ladies-maids lifted her train and she was told that when she reached the Cathedral there would be three pages to carry it.

A number of small bridesmaids hastily got together at the last moment would follow her up the aisle.

It had been assumed, that as the King was ill it would be some time before the wedding would actually take place.

Now everything had to be done within twenty-four hours.

Not only was everyone in the Palace breathless but it seemed as if the same applied to the town.

Lord Victor was standing very near her as she was helped into the carriage.

It had been drawn up as close to the door as possible.

There were soldiers on each side.

It would be impossible for anyone with any evil intention to kill her as she moved out of the Palace door and into the carriage.

Then Lord Victor joined her.

She slipped her hand in his.

"It is very exciting," she said.

She was thinking of the wedding that lay ahead.

He was looking from left to right, terrified that by some mischance a murdering Russian would at the last moment succeed where Alexander had failed.

The carriage set off.

On Lord Victor's instructions it moved more swiftly than anyone had expected.

There were Officers riding on either side of it and a large number in front and behind.

The road had been decorated as they had seen when they arrived at the Palace yesterday.

A great many more flags had been arranged earlier that morning.

A lot of the people especially the children carried either the flag of Zararis or a Union Jack.

They reached the Cathedral in what must have been record time.

This was another moment of which Lord Victor was afraid.

They had to climb up the steps of the Cathedral itself.

He had a guard of soldiers on either side and soldiers facing the crowds.

Yet there was still a possibility that a well-aimed bullet might hit the Princess.

When they were inside the Cathedral Lord Victor gave a sigh of relief and some of his tension left him.

The Bridesmaids looking like a bunch of rosebuds were waiting.

The pages in their satin clothes picked up the end of Princess Sydella's train as they had been told to do.

It was incorrect but Lord Victor had said to the Archbishop as well as to the General that he had no intention of waiting for his bride at the Chancel steps.

Instead of the English Ambassador who was to have given her away, he would walk with her up the aisle.

He had been very firm in his orders, very insistent that he should be obeyed.

In fact every man who had listened to him had gone away with the impression he would make an excellent King.

Things would soon start moving once he was on the Throne.

The Cathedral was packed even at such short notice.

People had been coming in from the country all night.

No-one in the whole country wanted to miss the most exciting and dramatic situation which had arisen in years.

They had all been shocked and appalled at the attempt to kill the Princess by blowing up the barge.

They thought that her courage like her beauty was everything they wanted as a Queen.

The King had never been popular.

They were therefore only too eager to accept

the exceedingly good-looking Englishman who had appeared at the very last moment and accepted the throne of Zararis.

The Princess and Lord Victor reached the Archbishop safely and the service began.

Lord Victor was however still afraid something might happen even in the Cathedral itself.

He had therefore insisted the marriage service was cut short so that they could start the Coronation.

As far as he and the Princess were concerned all that mattered was that they should be joined as man and wife.

They wanted also to receive the blessing of God who had already blessed them when they least expected it.

When they knelt for the blessing, Lord Victor was holding Sydella's hand.

He knew she was as deeply moved as he was.

He prayed as he had never prayed since he was a small boy that he would be able to protect her and make her happy.

He was entering a new world, a world of which he had little knowledge.

They had been saved from death by what seemed a miracle.

He could only believe that there was special work for them both to do and they would not fail the British Empire who relied on them.

When they rose to their feet the Coronation began.

After a flurry of trumpets which echoed and re-echoed round the whole building, Lord Victor knelt before the Archbishop.

He placed the crown on his head.

He then placed a smaller one on Princess Sydella's and blessed them both.

The trumpets sounded again and Lord Victor held out his hand to his Queen.

They were acclaimed by all those watching the ceremony in the Cathedral.

Especially by the nobility who were seated nearest to them and who wore the emblem of their importance.

It was then the Prime Minister and the members of the Council came forward to swear their allegiance to the King and Queen.

They did so on behalf of themselves and of the people of Zararis.

Once again they were acclaimed by all those present.

Then they walked down the aisle, while the ladies curtsied and the men bowed.

They reached the great West door.

Now the crowds had gathered until they stretched as far as the eye could see.

Just for a moment there was silence as their King and Queen stood in front of them.

Then they burst into wild cheers shouting their joy, flinging their hats into the air.

Their Majesties bowed in response until finally they moved down the steps.

There was a glittering gold coach drawn by six white horses to take them back to the Palace.

Now there was no need for the Cavalry to ride beside them and obscure them from the sight of their people.

Instead the windows were open and the Queen waved her hand, the King saluted.

They drove slowly back towards the Palace, the people cheering them all the way.

The children threw flowers into the carriage and in front of the horses.

It was the most noisy and triumphant journey imaginable.

It was impossible for either Sydella or Victor to speak to each other.

He was holding her right hand tightly in his and they were both pulsatingly aware that each other was there.

The cheers of the crowd seemed to echo and re-echo amongst the trees lining the route.

Those behind the Palace were brilliant with gold and silver baubles which glistened in the sunshine.

Because he thought it inappropriate, Lord Victor had insisted there would be no Banquet following the wedding and the Coronation.

That would be postponed out of respect for the late King for at least a month.

"It will be a great disappointment for those who would have been invited," the Prime Minister had protested.

"They will understand that we are mourning King Stephan," Lord Victor replied, "and also that my wife and I will want to be alone together."

The Prime Minister had therefore somewhat reluctantly agreed that Lord Victor should have his own way.

Now as King he thought it was something he intended to have for the rest of his life.

He was well aware that to build up Zararis the way the Marquess of Salisbury had wanted was almost a Herculean task.

However, it was what he intended to do.

He knew he would be helped in every way possible because Sydella was with them.

The adoring way she looked at him and her beauty would, he knew, make him strive for the well-being of the country to which he now belonged.

'I love her!' he told himself. 'And as long as she loves me, I will do great deeds and make Zararis a power in Europe simply so that I can lay every triumph at her feet.'

When they drove away from the Cathedral and she slipped her hand into his, he knew that no man could be more fortunate than to be her husband.

It was not only her exquisite beauty that was his but also her soul.

As they walked up red carpet covering the Palace steps, she said in a rapt little voice:

"How could I have known? How could I have guessed when I was so frightened yesterday that I would be so happy today? I feel as if the angels are all around us."

"That is what they are, my Lovely One," King Victor replied.

They were toasted as Their Majesties by their guests before they went upstairs to their apartments.

On King Victor's instructions they occupied the same rooms they had been allocated the night before.

He had decided not to move into the Royal Suite until it had been redecorated.

He did not want Sydella to think of anyone dying in the rooms in which they were to live.

She had no idea that Alexander had tried to murder her last night, or that Victor had foiled him.

He had called in the Officer in Charge of the men from H.M.S. *Victorious*.

Alexander's dead body had been hurriedly removed by them and disposed of.

No-one else was aware that anything untoward had happened.

"It would upset Her Royal Highness to know that her life had been threatened once again," Lord Victor had said. "I am therefore trusting all you men to speak of it to no-one.

"As he was wearing British uniform, it is not something of which we can be proud."

They had understood.

Lord Victor had closed the window in the Princess's bed-room and gone to his own room.

When Sydella awoke in the morning, she thought the night had passed without incident.

Nothing had happened to make her feel apprehensive on her Wedding Day.

Now as she went into the Sitting-Room, she gave a cry of joy.

Before they left for the Cathedral, Lord Victor had given an order to the Comptroller of the Household.

It was that every lily and every other variety of white flower available should be arranged in the Sitting-Room.

It made a bower of beauty and the fragrance of the blossoms filled the air.

King Victor shut the door behind them, pulled off his Coronation robe and set his crown down on a table.

The Queen was looking round the room.

"You . . you did this . . for me? Oh, Victor, it

is . . lovely . . and now I really feel . . that I am
. . married!"

He laughed as he replied:

"I am making certain of that! And now, my
beautiful Queen, I can tell you without any difficulties how much I love you."

She went towards him eagerly.

He took off her crown, which was a very pretty
one, and he thought no Queen could have looked
more beautiful.

Then he threw her long Coronation robe on the
floor and began to undo her elaborate white wed-
ding-gown.

"Wh . . what . . are you . . doing?"

"We are married, my Precious," the King
answered, "and after all I have suffered thinking I
had to lose you, I am wasting no more time before
teaching you, my beautiful, perfect little goddess,
about love."

"Oh, Darling, Darling, that is what I want,"
Sydella said, "but I thought I should have to . .
wait until . . tonight."

"We are not waiting for anything!" Victor declared. "We are starting our honeymoon from this
moment, and I have made it very clear that I wish
to be alone with you."

The gown dropped to the floor and as he removed
the hair-pins from her hair he said:

"Tomorrow there will be problems to solve, and
orders to be given. But until tomorrow this is our
glorious hour, and no-one shall disturb us."

"That is . . wonderful . . wonderful!" Sydella
whispered.

She thrilled as her husband lifted her up in

his arms and laid her gently down on the bed.

The sun coming through the open windows was dazzling.

She felt as if it was a special blessing sent by God.

Then as Victor joined her, she knew she was more blessed than any woman had ever been.

He drew her close to him.

She felt his hand touching her gently before his lips held hers captive.

The wonder and glory of it was part of the sunshine and the angels that had been with them in the Cathedral were singing.

It was then that Victor carried Sydella into a very special Heaven which lovers find only when they have passed through the perils of darkness.

They had found the love which comes from God, is part of God and is God.

It was theirs for Eternity.

Other books by Barbara Cartland

Romantic Novels, over 500, the most recently published being:

Running Away to Love
Look with the Heart
Safe in Paradise
Love in the Ruins
A Coronation of Love
A Duel of Jewels
The Duke is Trapped
Just a Wonderful Dream
Love and Cheetah
Drena and the Duke

A Dog, a Horse and a Heart
Never Lose Love
Spirit of Love
The Eyes of Love
The Duke's Dilemma
Saved by a Saint
Beyond the Stars
The Innocent Imposter
The Incomparable
The Dare-Devil Duke

The Dream and the Glory (In aid of the St. John Ambulance Brigade)

Autobiographical and Biographical:

The Isthmus Years 1919–1939
The Years of Opportunity 1939–1945
I Search for Rainbows 1945–1976
We Danced All Night 1919–1929
Ronald Cartland (With a foreword by Sir Winston Churchill)
Polly – My Wonderful Mother
I Seek the Miraculous

Historical:

Bewitching Women
The Outrageous Queen (The Story of Queen Christina of Sweden)
The Scandalous Life of King Carol
The Private Life of Charles II
The Private Life of Elizabeth, Empress of Austria
Josephine, Empress of France
Diane de Poitiers
Metternich – The Passionate Diplomat
A Year of Royal Days
Royal Jewels
Royal Eccentrics
Royal Lovers

Sociology:

You in the Home	Etiquette
The Fascinating Forties	The Many Facets of Love
Marriage for Moderns	Sex and the Teenager
Be Vivid, Be Vital	The Book of Charm
Love, Life and Sex	Living Together
Vitamins for Vitality	The Youth Secret
Husbands and Wives	The Magic of Honey
Men are Wonderful	The Book of Beauty and Health

Keep Young and Beautiful by Barbara Cartland and Elinor Glyn
Etiquette for Love and Romance
Barbara Cartland's Book of Health

General:

Barbara Cartland's Book of Useless Information with a Foreword by the
    Earl Mountbatten of Burma.
    (In aid of the United World Colleges)
Love and Lovers (Picture Book)
The Light of Love (Prayer Book)
Barbara Cartland's Scrapbook
(In aid of the Royal Photographic Museum)
Romantic Royal Marriages
Barbara Cartland's Book of Celebrities
Getting Older, Growing Younger

Verse:

Lines on Life and Love

Music:

An Album of Love Songs
sung with the Royal Philharmonic Orchestra

Films:

A Hazard of Hearts
The Lady and the Highwayman
A Ghost in Monte Carlo
A Duel of Hearts

Cartoons:

Barbara Cartland Romances (Book of Cartoons)
has recently been published in the U.S.A., Great Britain,
and other parts of the world.

Children:

A Children's Pop-Up Book: "Princess to the Rescue"

Videos:

A Hazard of Hearts
The Lady and the Highwayman
A Ghost in Monte Carlo
A Duel of Hearts

Cookery:

Barbara Cartland's Health Food Cookery Book
Food for Love
Magic of Honey Cookbook
Recipes for Lovers
The Romance of Food

Editor of:

"The Common Problem" by Ronald Cartland (with a preface by the Rt. Hon. the Earl of Selborne, P.C.)
Barbara Cartland's Library of Love
Library of Ancient Wisdom
"Written with Love" Passionate love letters selected by Barbara Cartland

Drama:

Blood Money
French Dressing

Philosophy:

Touch the Stars

Radio Operetta:

The Rose and the Violet
(Music by Mark Lubbock) Performed in 1942

Radio Plays:

The Caged Bird: An episode in the life of Elizabeth Empress of Austria Performed in 1957